REFUGEE TREASURE

Salaam

(p.69)

Books by Robert Elmer

PROMISE OF ZION

#1 / *Promise Breaker*
#2 / *Peace Rebel*
#3 / *Refugee Treasure*

ADVENTURES DOWN UNDER

#1 / *Escape to Murray River*
#2 / *Captive at Kangaroo Springs*
#3 / *Rescue at Boomerang Bend*
#4 / *Dingo Creek Challenge*
#5 / *Race to Wallaby Bay*
#6 / *Firestorm at Kookaburra Station*
#7 / *Koala Beach Outbreak*
#8 / *Panic at Emu Flat*

THE YOUNG UNDERGROUND

#1 / *A Way Through the Sea*
#2 / *Beyond the River*
#3 / *Into the Flames*
#4 / *Far From the Storm*
#5 / *Chasing the Wind*
#6 / *A Light in the Castle*
#7 / *Follow the Star*
#8 / *Touch the Sky*

ASTROKIDS

#1 / *The Great Galaxy Goof*
#2 / *The Zero-G Headache*
#3 / *Wired Wonder Woof*
#4 / *Miko's Muzzy Mess*

PROMISE *of* ZION 3

REFUGEE TREASURE

ROBERT ELMER

BETHANY HOUSE PUBLISHERS
MINNEAPOLIS, MINNESOTA 55438

Published by Bethany House Publishers
A Ministry of Bethany Fellowship International
11400 Hampshire Avenue South
Bloomington, Minnesota 55438
www.bethanyhouse.com

Printed in the United States of America by
Bethany Press International, Bloomington, Minnesota 55438

Library of Congress Cataloging-in-Publication Data

Elmer, Robert.
    Refugee treasure / by Robert Elmer.
        p.   cm. — (Promise of Zion ; 3)
    Summary: In 1947 two teenagers from different backgrounds are thrown
together once again as the United Nations votes to create the state of Israel.
    ISBN 0-7642-2299-6 (pbk.)
    1. Palestine—History—1917–1948—Juvenile fiction. [1. Palestine—
History—1917–1948—Fiction. 2. Refugees, Jewish—Fiction. 3. Christian
life—Fiction.] I. Title.
PZ7.E4794 Rd   2001
[Fic]—dc21   00-012158

To Rochelle and Peter—

Two are better than one; because they have a good reward for their labour.

—Eccelesiastes 4:9

ROBERT ELMER is the author of several other series for young readers, including ADVENTURES DOWN UNDER and THE YOUNG UNDERGROUND. He got his writing start as a newspaper reporter but has written everything from magazine columns to radio and TV commercials. Now he writes full-time from his home in rural northwest Washington state, where he lives with his wife, Ronda, and their three busy teenagers.

CONTENTS

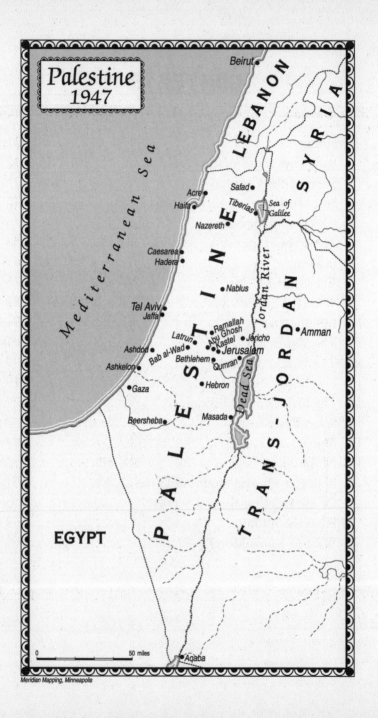

Palestine
1947

Meridian Mapping, Minneapolis

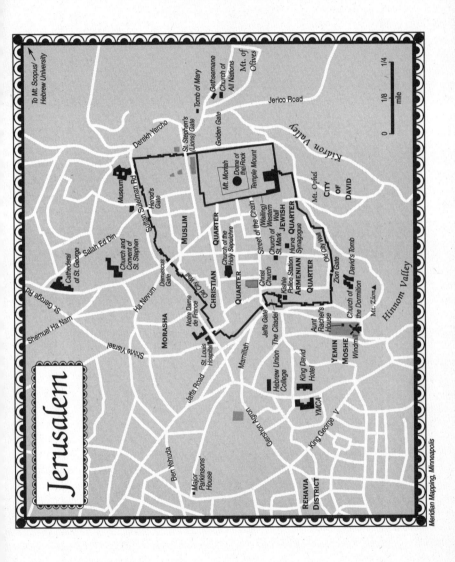

Jerusalem

To Mt. Scopus/
Hebrew University

Derekh Yercho

Tomb of Mary
St. Stephen's
(Lions) Gate

Gethsemane
Church of
All Nations

Mt. of
Olives

Jerico Road

Golden Gate

Kidron Valley

Museum

Sultan Suleiman Rd

Herod's
Gate

MUSLIM

QUARTER

Mt. Moriah

Dome of
the Rock

Temple Mount

Mt. Ophel

CITY
OF
DAVID

Salah Ed Din

Cathedral
of St. George

Church and
Convent of
St. Stephen

St. George Rd

Shemuel Ha Nam

Ha Nevum

Damascus
Gate

Old City Wall

Notre Dame
de France

Church of the
Holy Sepulchre

CHRISTIAN

QUARTER

Street of the Chain

Church of Western
(Wailing)
Wall

St. Mark

JEWISH
QUARTER

Hurva
Synagogue

Old City Wall

Christ
Church

Kishle
Police Station

ARMENIAN
QUARTER

Zion Gate

David's Tomb

Shivte Yisrael

Shmuel Ha Nam

MORASHA

Jaffa Gate

The Citadel

Jafa Road

St. Louis
Hospital

Mamillah

Aunt
Rachel's
House

Church of
the Dormition

Mt. Zion

Hinnom Valley

YEMIN
MOSHE

Windmill

Ben Yehuda

Major
Parkinsons'
House

Gershon Agron

Hebrew Union
College

King David
Hotel

YMCA

King George V

REHAVIA
DISTRICT

0   1/8   1/4

mile

Meridian Mapping, Minneapolis

HUNGRY

Jerusalem
September 28, 1947

"Watch out, lad!"

Dov Zalinski must have jumped a foot in the air when a glass bottle shattered into a million pieces at his feet. Wicked shards of green glass skittered off to his left across uneven Jerusalem cobblestones.

Close. But who had warned him? He turned to see—at just the wrong time.

The older Arab man coming out of his door probably didn't see Dov. And he probably didn't mean to bowl Dov into the middle of the narrow street in front of the two soldiers. Within a moment, the Arab in the flowing white robe and traditional black *kaffiyeh* headdress had disappeared into the shadows.

Dov lay sprawled on his back, looking up into two ruddy English faces.

"You all right?" The younger of the two soldiers bent down and held out his hand to help Dov up. He couldn't have been more than five or six years older than Dov's thirteen.

Dov didn't need the help, thank you very much. He held

his hand close to his chest and stayed where he was.

"Suit yourself." The soldier shrugged. "Only don't blame us when you get hurt, wandering around like a tourist."

Not that Dov didn't want to move. Besides the broken glass, the street was damp, and it smelled terrible. But he would not accept help from these soldiers. The men wore the same khaki uniforms and jaunty red berets he had seen before on the Jewish refugee ship, the *Aliyah*. It still made Dov's blood boil when he remembered how he and the other Jews had been stopped and their ship boarded not even two weeks ago—by soldiers just like this. And within sight of *Eretz Israel*, the Promised Land!

"Forget about the boy, Jenkins," the leader barked. "Just keep an eye out."

Good idea—they had to know the bottle was meant for them. Dov noticed the young soldier's finger twitching dangerously close to the trigger of his weapon. That kept Dov frozen where he was. The tip of the soldier's rifle shook a little, but still it hung ready, pointed at the damp cobblestones of the narrow market street.

The rifle would not be enough to protect them here. Even before the bottle had come flying out of nowhere, Dov had noticed eyes all around—dark eyes in doorways, behind faded curtains and dusky windowpanes. It was no surprise to see the pale glimmer of sweat on the faces of the young soldiers.

Even behind their set jaws and tight lips, Dov could make out the sure signs of fear. He'd seen it before—in a prisoner's eyes, back in the Nazi camp, before the war had ended. And here another war was already beginning.

"Right." Jenkins' voice quivered a bit as he backed away. "Let's be off, then."

Dov used the moment of doubt to roll clear and scramble

to his feet. Never mind his ripped pants and hurt knee. He had no idea where he would go, only knew he would breathe much easier when he was far away from these two.

One thing they were right about—he *had* been wandering about the old market street like a tourist. A tourist? The idea was almost funny.

But if not a tourist, then he was surely a stranger. Someone who didn't speak or understand the strange musical words floating out the doorways, over the piles of green melons, and around the smoking brass water pipes with strange, octopus-like tubes.

An Arab woman in an embroidered dress pushed past him, balancing an overflowing basket of fruit on her head.

He had never known such a strange symphony of smells, curious and peculiar and wonderful all at the same time. For a moment it seemed he would burst if he tried to take it all in.

"Bandura, bandura!" cried a man watching over several baskets of pungent, rotting tomatoes. The smell slapped Dov's nose. Next to him a woman in a dark, filmy veil guarded garlic and cucumbers, grape leaves, squash, and eggplant. The weird smells of fresh dill and parsley played tag with heavy aromas of leather and spice, strong coffee and dust, surely borne here on the back of a camel, a caravan from where? Dov could hardly begin to guess as he followed his nose through this tangle of smells and shouts and sights and sounds.

What kind of incredible, ancient city had he traveled so far to see? He'd found his way from Warsaw, through the bombed-out rail yards of Germany, over the Alps to Italy, across the Mediterranean, and all the way to Palestine. But nothing had prepared him for this, the Old City of Jerusalem. Probably he was going in circles in a maze of strange streets barely wide enough for three people to walk shoulder to shoulder; he thought he recognized the front of a brass merchant's shop, lined with shining brass pitchers on both walls. Slivers of late-morning light filtered through the rising smoke gathering in vaulted ceilings.

Dov was pretty sure this street was on some kind of lower level, like a basement—one that acted like a mixing bowl of very strange, smoky smells. A man in a traditional Arab headdress squatted next to a small brazier of smoking meat. The lifting smoke again drew Dov's gaze to the vaulted ceiling, where dark stains told him that someone had been cooking lunch in that spot for a very long time.

Dov closed his eyes and felt his mouth water, and when he breathed in he wished the smell and the smoke could stop his stomach from rumbling. He could only keep going, pretending he had somewhere to go, someone to buy groceries for. Dark-haired men sat on wooden folding chairs in the openings to their shop-caves, smoking tiny stubs of cigarettes and staring at him as if he had no right to be wandering in their maze.

Maybe he didn't. He ducked under a red-and-gold tapestry hanging from a pole and nearly tripped over a collection of burlap sacks bulging out from the doors of another shop. The young boy tending the shop eyed him carefully, and Dov nodded as if he came this way every day. The boy said nothing, and Dov paused for a moment, suddenly overwhelmed by the heady smell of spices.

Saffron, Dov read on the little cardboard sign stuck into the mustard-yellow powder. Under the English, he recognized graceful swirls and curls as Arabic writing, though of course he couldn't make out any of the foreign letters. *Curry* in another sack, *Cumin* in the next. And on and on, a nose-numbing collection of yellow and orange and burnt-brown powders, crushed bark, and maybe just plain dirt, for all he knew. *Pepper, black.* Dov turned away to sneeze . . . once . . . twice . . . three times. The spice boy frowned at him, so Dov kept going, up and around another corner, to a wider lane, then up some stairs.

Where am I? Not that it mattered, but he looked for a street marker. Was that it? *Ha Shal-shelet,* the Street of the Chain. So said in two languages the white tile sign set into the ancient stone wall above his head.

Keep walking, he told himself, and still he looked for familiar words on the unfamiliar signs. For the friendly, strong Hebrew letters that would tell him he was finally in the right place. He'd heard there were Muslim and Christian Quarters of the city, Armenian and Jewish, too. Only, which was where? Because in the Jewish Quarter would be synagogues, and in the synagogues would be rabbis, and maybe, just maybe, the rabbis could tell him if his family had made it here from Poland, as they'd said they would, back before the war. But that was years ago. What had happened to his family, to *Abba* and *Imma,* his father and mother?

Where are you? He hit a metal roll-up door with the side of his fist and closed his eyes. He would not cry—not here in this foreign place. Instead, he tried to remember once again what his father had told him, what his mother had sung to him. But no matter how hard he tried, still he could not remember their faces. Not Abba and Imma, not his older brother. Just their names—his older brother, Natan, his mother, Leah, and his father, Mordecai Zalinski.

Where was the Jewish Quarter? Here in this neighborhood all the words he saw were Arabic, sometimes with English underneath.

Kabab and Sheshlak, declared one sign, block letters on a simple wooden board hanging from a wire attached to the ceiling. Dov's nose told him that would be food, and again his stomach reminded him that he had not eaten since . . . had it been a day and a night? He wasn't sure.

The Golden Rock Factory for Olive Wood, said another sign, hand-lettered in English on the edge of a rusty metal roof overhang. That didn't sound like food, but then again . . . He smelled the rich spices and the fresh bread before he saw them, the aroma guiding him to the neat, full baskets nailed to the inside of an open blue door. Obviously the Golden Rock Factory for Olive Wood dealt in more than just olive wood.

And a good thing, too. Desperately good. Dov wandered in behind a woman with a dark shawl over her head. A wicker shopping basket dangled from her arm; a barefoot boy with a runny nose hung on to the fringe of her skirt. And Dov could not shake the temptation that lurked in the back of his mind—no matter how he tried.

I shouldn't. He wondered at the voice in his head, wondered why it was suddenly so hard to just slip the bread into his shirt and walk away. It would be that easy. He had lived that way during the war, back in the camps. He had survived, hadn't he?

The shopkeeper didn't seem to notice as he chatted with the woman, waving his hands and laughing. It would be now, or not at all. Dov could nearly taste the bread, and he knew it would be horribly good. . . .

As if it were a heavy weight, he pushed the unfamiliar *no* out of his mind, glanced one last time at the back of the shopkeeper's bald head, and slipped three crusty sesame-seed rolls into the folds of his shirt.

BAD NEWS AND WORSE

"Oh!" Emily Parkinson smiled and leaned over the dining table. "I'd almost forgotten how grand this fresh bread smells. Ginger, it's heavenly. Ginger?"

She looked up, expecting to see the smiling housekeeper who had served almost as a second mother all these years. Instead, she looked straight into the black eyes of a dark-haired Arab woman, who looked quickly away. The woman wore the same prim light blue, ankle-length dress Ginger had always worn, and her shining black hair was pulled back into a bun.

"Oh—terribly sorry. Is Ginger. . . ?"

"We meant to tell you, Emily," began her mother. She dabbed properly at the corner of her mouth with a white linen napkin. "But it was just too much . . . all at once. We didn't want you to worry."

The way her mother chewed on the words told Emily that all was not well, that perhaps Ginger didn't just have the day off.

"Where is she?" Emily looked past the retreating servant

and through the swinging kitchen door. No Ginger. "Mother?"

"It was for the best," sighed Mrs. Parkinson.

Emily waited to hear more.

"She decided it was time to return home," explained Emily's father. "Another group of civilians was being evacuated to our base in Cairo. And, given the circumstances, we did nothing to dissuade her. You understand, dear. I daresay she's safer now."

"What?" Emily couldn't believe what she was hearing. "You didn't order her to stay?"

"Emily, you know that this is a dangerous time in Palestine, and . . ."

Emily closed her eyes. She had heard it all before. Still, she tried to pretend their home hadn't become an armed fort, almost, with the security zones and the extra guards outside.

". . . we're one of the few families who haven't evacuated with the rest. I've been criticized by everyone for keeping you here in Jerusalem."

"I know that, Daddy. But Ginger . . . she's part of the family! And she didn't even say good-bye."

How could they do this? Emily had so been looking forward to seeing her old friend. Now there was no telling how long it would be before she saw her again. Julian, her aging tan-and-black Great Dane, nuzzled her knee for a handout from his place under the table. She lowered him a piece of bread dipped in brown gravy, which he gladly inhaled.

"Alan, do you think perhaps we made a mistake . . . ?" Emily's mother bit her lip, but her father shook his head and held up his hand.

"We've been over this many times, dear."

"Yes, but Emily . . . especially after what's happened."

"I'm not saying you and Em can't return home, as well, Violet. Personally, I'd welcome it—knowing you're safe, and all. It's just my conviction that—"

"I know." Mrs. Parkinson nodded. "It's not just you, remember. I was the one who insisted we stay together last spring, when everyone else was leaving."

"That's my girl," declared the major. "Can't let them imagine they've won, now, can we?"

Emily knew her father's next words by heart.

"Stiff upper lip and all that."

She never could figure out what lips had to do with being brave, especially not *upper* lips. *Lower* lips, perhaps. Even worse, Emily wasn't quite sure who was winning or losing, or even who "they" were, anymore. Were "they" the Jewish terrorists who had held her prisoner for two long days? Maybe "they" were the settlers back at *Kibbutz Yad Shalom*, who wanted only to be left alone to farm their rocky lands. Or that cheeky Jewish boy, Dov Zalinski, who had joined a group of American students to help her escape. Or how about the Arabs who lived all around them in Jerusalem, like the woman who now served their dinner?

"Her name is Wardi." Mrs. Parkinson must have noticed Emily's glance at the kitchen door. "I was told she's a marvelous cook. And you know better than to feed Julian at the table."

"Yes, Mum."

Tears flooded Mrs. Parkinson's eyes when she looked at Emily.

"I'm perfectly all right." Emily almost blushed. "God was taking care of me, remember? Just as you always tell me He is."

"I know, dear." Emily's mother leaned across the table and

rested her hand on her daughter's. "I know. But I will tell you one thing for certain: I am not going to let you out of my sight from now on."

"Mother," Emily sighed. "Don't forget, I'm thirteen, remember?"

Emily's mother laughed, and it sounded good. "Thirteen, thirty, a hundred and three, you'll always be my baby. And I'm going to make sure nothing like . . . that . . . ever happens again."

"I don't expect it will." Major Parkinson wiped the corner of his mouth with a linen napkin and pushed his soup bowl to the side. "Our boys picked up all three of the kidnappers, so you won't have to worry about *them*, in any case. And if it's the last thing I do, I am going to see they're dealt with most severely."

"Oh." Emily wondered what "most severely" might mean. Not that it was right, what the terrorists had done. Dressed as British soldiers, they'd kidnapped her out of the kibbutz in broad daylight, for goodness' sake. Better not to think about it anymore. Her father went on as if he were briefing his staff—which Emily tended to think she and her mother were sometimes.

"Two of them were picked up in Ashkelon, and the other one in that little kibbutz, er . . ."

"Yad Shalom." Emily wouldn't soon forget the Jewish farm. "Where they took me the night I was pushed off the ship."

"Yes, of course." The major nodded his head and looked more thoughtful. "And I quite blame myself for allowing that entire ugly incident to happen. Fortunately, they didn't dare harm a British subject."

"And now, Miss British Subject, we have you back again."

Emily's mother finished the thought with a smile. "So that's the way it's going to stay until . . ." She looked at her husband. "How long, now, Alan, before we'll return home?"

"Home?" Emily pretended not to understand, but she knew exactly where this conversation was going. "We *are* home."

"No, dear," her mother corrected her. "I mean home to Kent, of course. Parkinson Manor."

"But I hardly *remember* that place," complained Emily. "And Ginger says—or she *said*—it was rainy and gloomy and drafty."

"Don't you recall the fields you used to play in with your little friend . . . what was his name?"

Billy Custer, thought Emily. She pressed her lips together.

"Well, never mind. I'm certain you'll make new friends." Mrs. Parkinson forced a brave smile.

"I'll keep my old ones if we stay here." But Emily wasn't quite sure whom she was talking about. Most of her school friends had already left the country. Of course, there was always her aunt Rachel. She would never leave Jerusalem, either, just like Emily. They would never leave the glorious city, the hills that seemed to sing to her, the ancient streets, the desert flowers that she loved. "And there's good old Julian, of course."

"Yes . . . well." Her mother glanced quickly at Major Parkinson, then traced a pattern around the rose on her linen napkin with the tip of her fork. "We've been meaning to speak with you about that, dear. Your father and I had thought that by now the problem would have . . . taken care of itself. Alan?"

"What problem?" Emily sat up straight. She found no clues in her father's face. He seemed taken up with a pile of reports just then. He gave her a quick sideways glance.

"Your mother is talking about the dog, Emily."

"Yes, but he's no problem. Julian is—"

"Julian is nearing the end of his days, Emily." Finally Major Parkinson put down his papers. "He wasn't much more than a puppy when we dragged him here. I know how much that old beast means to you, but you must know he's too old to travel back home. Simply too old."

The thought of leaving her dog behind had never occurred to Emily before. Not for an instant. And if she had been a year younger, she would have been tempted to plug her ears and run from the room, sobbing. Now she did her best to keep her voice from quivering.

"Well, then, we'll just have to stay." Emily hoped somehow that saying it often enough would make it true. "We will."

"Precisely what your mother and I were getting at." The major pushed out his chair and stood.

Emily always thought he looked handsome in his pressed army uniform—the trim khaki tan coat with the shoulder boards, the neat, colorful row of square service medals across the top of his left chest pocket, and the bright embroidered shoulder patch of the Eighty-seventh Airborne Regiment. Only now she couldn't see it through a blurry curtain of warm tears.

"Where are you going, Alan?" Mrs. Parkinson asked.

"I haven't been able to explain everything to you until now," he told them over his shoulder. "Quite confidential, you see. But I believe they're going to make an announcement tonight on the BBC. The radio broadcast."

Less than an hour later, Emily was hearing more than she wanted to know, as the official voice of the British Broadcasting Corporation's nightly radio announcement for Sunday, September 28, 1947, filled their sitting room with news from around the world.

Emily sat with her fingers knotted in her lap, waiting for the report her father said would explain everything. They sat through a report of a cholera epidemic in Egypt, and an update on the riots in New Delhi between the Sikhs and Hindus against the Muslims. More Jewish refugees had been forced back to Europe. Emily noticed Wardi's shadow in the kitchen, standing statue-still, listening with them, waiting for the news about Palestine.

> "In a long-awaited British statement of policy, Colonial Secretary Arthur Creech Jones told the fifty-five-member Special Committee on Palestine of the UN yesterday in Lake Success, New York, that Britain intends to abandon the twenty-five-year-old mandate over Palestine and pull out her military and government forces in the area by what he called 'an early date.'"

Emily closed her eyes. So it was true. Her father was right. The British were really leaving.

"Does that mean—"

"Shh!" Major Parkinson wanted to hear the rest of the broadcast, but Emily didn't care about all the details, about what the committee chairman said, or about how the Arabs and Jews were arguing now about what to do after the British ran for home. Or even about the rumors that a Jewish state would be formed. And finally . . .

"In other news, four people were injured in Tel Aviv last night when a bank—"

Major Parkinson reached over and snapped off the big mahogany Philips radio. There, that was it.

"Is *that* what you couldn't tell us?" whispered Emily's mother.

The major nodded.

"What did he mean by 'an early date'?"

Major Parkinson rubbed his rather pointed chin, thinking. "Six months. Eight. No more. We'll be home in England almost as soon as you can pack your bags."

Emily's mother was beaming until she caught sight of Emily's stormy expression. "It's really for the best, dear."

Again Emily pressed her lips together, afraid to say anything.

Her father looked at her curiously.

"I had no idea you'd take it so badly." He stood back up. "In fact, I've made some inquiries, and it seems they have an opening at a proper girl's finishing school not far from home. Willingdon Academy."

"What?" This was more than Emily could take. First Ginger. Then Julian and leaving. And now a *finishing school*?

"Classes have already started, to be sure, but under the circumstances they'd be willing to accept you midterm."

A nightmare. This had to be a nightmare. Soon she would wake up.

But her father continued. "I know your mother promised you we'd stay together," he said, "but things have become quite dangerous here in Palestine."

"No!" Emily did her best not to burst out in tears. "Mrs. DeBoer is a fine tutor."

Or at least, Mrs. DeBoer the tutor was better than what her parents were suggesting. Anything would be better than leaving Jerusalem. Emily would learn how to understand the woman's heavy Dutch accent better. She would have to.

But her father had other ideas. "Mrs. DeBoer has informed us she will be leaving Palestine before the end of the year, and that we should make other arrangements for your schooling, effective immediately."

Emily's sails lost their wind, and she could find nothing else to say. Could her parents throw any more bad news her way? She lifted herself out of the flowered sofa and shuffled for the door.

"We'll talk about it again soon, dear," her mother crooned. "Get some sleep. Go to bed early. You'll feel better about it in the morning."

Emily nodded, but she knew she wouldn't. She snapped her fingers. "Julian. Here, boy."

For a moment, she almost wished she hadn't been rescued. Or perhaps she could have stayed with that obnoxious Dov Zalinski—who probably still thought he could find his long-lost parents here in Jerusalem, all by himself.

STREET OF THE
CHAIN
3

"*Harami!*" shouted the shopkeeper. "Harami!"

Dov needed no translation to know what the cry meant. *Stop* or *thief*, one or the other. But it was too late for language lessons. He looked quickly down the street for a way to escape, a crowd to disappear behind, an alley with plenty of shadows to blend into.

Once again, his timing was off. A delivery boy chose that time to push his three-wheeled cart by the store, full to the brim with watermelons and close enough to the door to clip Dov's feet.

"Oh!" Dov pulled back for an instant, which was good for not bowling over the watermelons, but not so good to avoid being caught by the angry shopkeeper. A moment later Dov was gasping for breath, hanging by his collar like a just-caught fish on a string. The shopkeeper with eyes in the back of his head held him up to dry.

I've never known anyone with such strong hands, thought Dov, and there was no question about getting away.

He just wondered which wall he would be hung up on, a

hunting trophy like the one he had seen once in a book. Dov practically saw steam rising from the top of the man's bald head.

But he was not completely bald, this shopkeeper. The middle-aged man sported brave shocks of wiry hair on each side of his head, bright silver against his golden-bronze skin, matched by silver caterpillars above his eyes. His chin was shaved clean, and he was neatly dressed in a merchant's white shirt and plain black pants with careful creases. The man was almost old enough to be Dov's grandfather, and he stood a half head taller. But judging by the way he held Dov in the air, his arms weren't like an older man's at all. More like the tough, braided rope used to tie up ships.

Naturally Dov could not understand a word of the man's lecture. He didn't need to. The language of an angry wagging finger was more than enough. The stern fire in the man's dark eyes was simple to understand, too.

"Harami," repeated the man several times, as if he expected an answer. Then another jumble of gargled words, a question Dov could not answer. The shopkeeper paused for breath, which gave Dov a chance to remember the strange, insisting voice in his head again, the "no" he had ignored. By this time he was sure he would rather have stayed hungry awhile longer than be scolded by the Arab shopkeeper's harsh-sounding words.

I'm such a fool. But what could he do about it now? He'd let his stomach do his thinking for him. Sesame seeds had slipped down from his shirt into his pants. All he could think of was the bread, so he rolled up one sleeve, reached into his shirt, and held the rolls out to the man. Never mind that Muslims cut off the hands of thieves. He'd heard that back on the ship, along with plenty of other stories about these people.

"I am sorry," he whispered in English. "I was hungry." It was no excuse, of course, but the six words stopped the flood of Arabic like a hot desert wind dried up a rain. The two of them stared at each other for a long, uneasy moment.

"You're a . . ." the man finally whispered, this time in English. He glanced at the tattooed number on Dov's forearm. "You're a Jew."

He continued to hold Dov at arm's length by the shoulders. It hurt.

Dov opened his mouth but nothing came out. Of course, a fish with a hook in its mouth couldn't speak, either.

"You should know better than to wander along Ha Shalshelet. Jews are no longer welcome on Arab streets."

"I didn't know anything about Hash el . . ." Dov stumbled over his first try at the Arabic words. They did not roll off his tongue the way he'd hoped.

"Ha Shal-shelet," the man corrected him. "The Street of the Chain."

"Street of the Chain, of course." That was much easier to say, but he wasn't fooling anyone.

"So you're new to the city, eh? What's your name, little thief? Little harami?"

So that's what the word meant. Harami. Thief. Dov swallowed hard. It didn't seem wise to disobey this man with the strong hands and the sharp eyes.

The shopkeeper relaxed his grip and looked at Dov as if for the first time—at the wild black hair that had not been cut for a month and a half; the ragged yellow hand-me-down shirt he had been given at the kibbutz; and the well-ventilated trousers sewn many years ago for a man who had eaten many more meals than he, now held up by a rope around Dov's waist.

"And look at you. What does your mother think of you roaming the streets, stealing bread from Farouk Bin-Jazzi's shop, eh? Do you know what Muslims do to the hands of thieves?"

Dov winced when Mr. Farouk Bin-Jazzi made a chopping motion with one hand into the other palm.

"I . . . I don't know where my parents are. I came to find them. We're from Poland. My name is Dov Zalinski."

Farouk Bin-Jazzi caught his breath and studied him carefully. "At night, then, Dov Zalinski, where do you stay? Your knee is hurt."

Dov said nothing, just studied his shoes, the worn brown leather shoes that would have fit a much larger man perfectly. Newspaper stuffed in the toes helped, and no one could see *that*. He was at least glad the fire in this man's eyes had died down to bright embers. Mr. Bin-Jazzi's hands were just as strong, though, as he led Dov to the back room. He did not take back the bread.

"I should have guessed. All right, then. You sit here. Wait."

Dov found a seat on a carved mahogany stool, wedged in under a set of lopsided shelves loaded with brass candlesticks and olive-wood carvings—camels and manger scenes, mostly. A few crosses hung on the wall, inlaid with pretty white ivory or mother-of-pearl. And back in the shadows of the room, he squinted at bigger objects—dusty, dark shapes he couldn't quite make out. He heard shuffling in the front room behind a faded red curtain with gold tassels along the bottom fringe, low talking, then nothing for several minutes.

He's probably gone to sharpen his cleaver.

As Dov waited, the larger, tarp-covered shapes in the corners seemed to waken and move like the monsters Dov had imagined as a boy growing up in the orphanage. Back then, the monsters lived under his mattress and in the creaky wardrobes set up beside each bed. Dov thought he had left all that behind, back in the Land That Was Destroyed, the place where the war had been. Had he discovered another war here? What kind of Promised Land was this?

Dov dried the sweat from his palms and wondered what to do with the three rolls he'd stolen. Eat them now? Put them back on the shelf, next to the brass candlesticks? That seemed silly, but he didn't understand why the shopkeeper hadn't taken them back. And what had happened to this Mr. Farouk Bin-Jazzi? Dov started to get up when he heard the curtain swishing.

"Sit down and wait, I said, Dov Zalinski!" ordered Mr. Bin-Jazzi.

Dov blinked at the light coming in from the street; it framed the shopkeeper like one of Dov's monsters. Actually, bright sunlight behind the man's square shoulders made him look like a pocket-sized wrestler. Dov sneezed on the roll that he gripped in his hand. Perhaps it could still be sold . . . at a lower price.

"Did you call the police?" Dov asked, and he wondered what kind of food he might get in jail. For just a moment, the thought of jail food didn't seem all bad. But only for a moment.

"The police?" Mr. Bin-Jazzi chuckled for the first time. He set a tray down next to Dov on a low, small table. No cleaver—just three bowls next to a mug of water. "No, but perhaps I should have. Here." He pointed at the tray. "Here is something for you to eat. You are hungry, are you not?"

Dov's eyes widened when he realized what Mr. Bin-Jazzi had brought him. One bowl held dates and a few dried figs.

The other, strips of cold meat, and the third, a sort of curdled, lumpy white cheese he had never tasted before. It had a sour bite, but no matter. He had never tasted better food in his life.

Mr. Bin-Jazzi described his store while Dov ate, or rather, inhaled the food. "You noticed the bread in front," said the man. "People stop for the bread . . . to *buy*, that is. I have other things, as well. A small pharmacy for the aches and pains. For stomach ailments and infections, too. A bit of food, some groceries, a few spices. Olive-wood crafts my sister's husband makes in Bethlehem. Brass candlesticks, the same as you can find in a hundred other shops here in the Old City. But *this* . . ."

He paused and swept his hand across the dark room. The monsters in the corners.

"This is my *real* place of business. Farouk Bin-Jazzi deals in the finest of antiquities. Swords from the Crusades and Byzantine times. Herodian tapestries. Roman coins. Even ancient pottery and scrolls from the Iron Age. My customers come to *me* for honest dealing. They know I won't steal from anyone."

Dov knew the last comment was meant for him. He ate another roll, piled high with the strong-smelling cheese.

"Yes, go ahead, finish your stolen bread, my little thief. The dates, as well." Mr. Bin-Jazzi crossed his arms and seemed to enjoy watching Dov inhale the food. "But don't eat the pits."

"What pits?" asked Dov as he finished the last of the wonderful, wonderful dates.

"Hmph. Well, no matter. They won't hurt you. And neither will the work you're about to do."

He found a straw broom in the corner and held it out to Dov.

"You will sweep from the back to the front. And when you're finished with that, I have plenty of other chores for you. Straightening shelves. Running errands. I'll teach you some Arabic so people here in the neighborhood won't bother you as much. Some of it is like Hebrew. And there's a cot here in the back room for you to sleep on until you find your family."

Dov wasn't quite sure what he was hearing. But he stood and took the broom, covering a satisfied burp.

" 'Let him that stole steal no more,' " said the man, " 'rather let him labor, working with his hands the thing which is good.' You wouldn't know who said that, but in my shop you will live by such a saying."

"From your holy book?" asked Dov. He knew the Arabs had their own book, their own places of worship, the places with the high towers scattered around the city. Even from the outside, they looked very different from what he knew of Jewish synagogues.

"The apostle Paul." The shopkeeper started toward the front room to meet a customer. He paused at the curtain and looked over his shoulder. "I am a Christian, not a Muslim. My father was a Maronite, and his father before him. But I'll tell you something."

He paused for effect, and once more made a chopping motion with his hand. "If you ever steal from me again, Dov Zalinski . . ."

"I'll sweep, sir."

Dov shivered and turned to his chore. He still wasn't sure about this Mr. Farouk Bin-Jazzi, if he could trust him, or what would happen if he did. But what choice did he have? For now he would sweep, clean, do what this man told him to do. He understood the warning, though he wasn't quite sure if the shopkeeper was serious.

He was sure of one thing, though: *I don't want to find out.*

STILL MISSING

4

"So all you can tell me is that this Mr. and Mrs. Zaleski may be from Warsaw, Poland." The young woman behind the counter sighed as she flipped back a stray strand of dark hair, licked her fingertip, and leafed through her thick ledger book. Perhaps she'd had a long day.

"Zal-IN-ski," Emily corrected her. "Mr. and Mrs. Mordecai Zalinski."

"Zalinski, Zawoyski, Za-who-ski . . . Honestly, dear. Do you know how many hundreds of refugees we're dealing with every day? Both legal *and* illegal, I mean."

"Quite a few, I'm sure."

"Ha! Quite a few, you say." The woman dropped a thick binder of papers on the counter with a thud, careful not to chip her red-painted nails. "Here's today's. Look—Wednesday, and it's not yet three o'clock. Six hundred and thirty-two names. Tomorrow we'll probably see another five hundred, and the next day, and the next. All of them with horribly impossible names."

Emily nodded politely and let the woman complain.

"Heaven only knows why they try to sneak here on their decrepit ships. They'd be much better off if they would just stay in Europe, where they came from."

"Mm-hmm."

"We just turn them back or take them to detention centers on the island of Cyprus."

"Prison camps?"

"I said 'detention centers,' young lady. Not camps."

"I see." But Emily did not. "You have records of those names, the people sent to the . . . centers?"

"You don't understand." The woman scowled. "Keeping track of all these horrid names is an administrative nightmare."

"Hmm." Emily honestly wasn't sure why she was searching for Dov's parents. After all, her father was expecting her in his upstairs office in a few minutes. Why did she care so much about finding these strangers?

"Couldn't you please check again?" Emily pointed to the form she had pushed across the counter. She wondered where her friend Francine was, who usually worked here and who actually smiled. "It's Zalinski. *I-n-s-k-i.* They could have arrived here anytime after the war. My father, Major Parkinson, says—"

"I *know* your father works upstairs and gives orders to quite a few people in this building." The woman leveled her gaze at Emily. "But in this case, my dear, I'm afraid that doesn't help matters in the least."

"I didn't mean it that way. I only meant to say—"

"Oh, I know exactly what you meant." The clerk slammed her ledger shut with a thump and a frown. "And as far as the Zalooskis are concerned, if they had entered the country *legally*, perhaps we'd have their names by now. But I'm not seeing them here."

"Perhaps you could have Francine check for me. She always—"

"Francine doesn't work here anymore," snapped the clerk. "Unfortunately, I do. Now, if you please."

"What happened to her?"

"Reassigned to Cairo, I hear." The young woman smiled bitterly, showing off a tea-stained set of front teeth that were a little too large for her mouth. "Which, I suppose, is a sight better than being abandoned *here*. But not much. They tell me the stench is dreadful in Cairo, and the flies bite horribly."

Emily shuddered at the thought of her friend working in a swarm of flies. She couldn't imagine why anyone would want to leave Jerusalem.

"And in case you haven't heard, Miss Parkinson, we British are not staying in this revolting little province. So a search of this sort is really none of your concern, nor is it mine. Thank goodness I, for one, am going home to London soon. You would be well advised to do the same. A pity, your father keeping you here, if you ask me."

"I just thought of something." Emily tried to ignore the woman's cranky words. "What if they're not exactly . . . legal?"

The woman raised her eyebrows. "Is there more to this story you're not telling me?"

"No, of course not. I was just thinking . . ."

"Thinking too much for your pretty head, if you ask me." Her eyes narrowed. "And by the way—these are friends of yours?"

"No, not exactly. He's rather, er, difficult, actually."

"Mr. Zalewski?"

"No. I mean Mr. Zalinski's son. His name is Dov. As far

as I know, he's here in Jerusalem."

"I see. Well, I suggest you tell this friend of yours that if he wants to locate his parents, he should inquire personally at the Jewish Agency. There's a Search Bureau for Missing Relatives on King George Street. I believe they keep track of their own people with a little more—" she cleared her throat—"enthusiasm than we do. If you quite understand my meaning."

Emily fingered the edge of the form she had filled out.

"So does this mean you can't check for me?"

"Check?" The woman nearly laughed and pointed at the nearby wall. "Look at that calendar, dear."

Emily didn't care for the way the woman said "dear," as if she meant exactly the opposite.

"It's Wednesday, October 1. That means I'm leaving in precisely two months, saints be praised. Now, does it appear to you as if we have the time to check?"

She waved her hand at a row of ten or twelve young ladies sitting at a long table, each one hammering at an ancient black Remington typewriter, probably left over from the last war. Assistants scurried around the office like ants at a picnic, ferrying papers and orders to who-knows-where. Of course, Emily's father's office had always been busy before. Now it was elbow to elbow with strangers, all in a panic.

"I suppose not." Emily wasn't sure anyone could hear her voice above the clatter.

"Please go home, Miss Parkinson." The woman sighed, looked past Emily, and motioned for the man behind her to step forward. "Next."

Of course, Emily didn't follow the tired clerk's advice. Her father would be waiting for her in his office upstairs. A minute later she paused outside his door, taking a deep breath. It would be only a few questions, he had told her that morning.

Nothing to be alarmed about. She knocked softly on the door and pushed her face into the room with a smile.

"Daddy?"

"Ah, there she is." Emily's father stood up from behind his desk, raising his hand in a friendly salute. The other two men rose to their feet, as well. One wore the four gold stripes of a captain on his uniform's shoulder pads; the other man, three. A lieutenant. Both lower in rank than her father.

"Emily, this is Captain Snodgrass from Special Affairs and my newly assigned aide, Lieutenant Phipps. Captain Snodgrass would just like to . . ."

. . . *ask me a few questions.* Emily knew.

"So this is the brave young girl who showed so much spunk." Lieutenant Phipps stepped forward with a smile and an outstretched hand. He was much younger than the other man, and his eyes seemed to dance with a friendly hello.

Emily couldn't help noticing his striking blond, almost bleached-looking hair. She missed his outstretched hand but managed to latch on to his little finger with a slight giggle.

"Glad to meet you, Emily."

She sat down quickly in one of her father's chairs before the other man could try to shake her hand, too. He had a red wart or something on his ear and looked about as sour as the lieutenant looked friendly.

"You know how fortunate you are to even *be* here, young lady." Captain Snodgrass gave her a disapproving stare. "Normally people taken hostage by terrorists do not so easily escape."

Emily tried to keep her eyes off the wart. This captain reminded her of a teacher Emily had once suffered under. But her father winked at her. It would be all right.

"Yes, sir."

The smiling Lieutenant Phipps leaned forward in his chair and picked up a flat pitcher-shaped pottery lamp from the corner of Major Parkinson's desk. "An interesting piece, don't you think, Emily? Did you find this somewhere around here? Roman period. See the shape? This is where they would light it, and—"

"I'm not here to study archaeology, Phipps," growled the captain.

"Of course not." Lieutenant Phipps smiled easily and set the pottery back down. "I was just trying to put us all at ease."

"Let's try to get this over with, shall we?" Captain Snodgrass obviously didn't believe in small talk. "Now, Miss Parkinson. Several days ago you were held hostage by Jewish terrorists, were you not?"

"Yes, sir. For two days." *Surely everyone in this room knows the story by now*, Emily thought.

"Two days." He paced the room. "Perhaps you could describe for us how this came to pass, if you would, please?"

Emily patiently told her story once more: how she had followed her father to the refugee ship, the horrible moment when she was pushed overboard by the crowd as the railing broke, how she was picked up on the shore by Jewish people from the kibbutz. Captain Snodgrass frowned and looked away as she explained how she was eventually taken by terrorists to the house in the coastal town of Ashkelon, where she'd spent two horrid days before being rescued by Dov and his friends.

But that was another story—one that Captain Snodgrass hardly seemed to hear. Indeed, by this time he didn't look as if he was listening to her at all. Instead, he turned his attention to Emily's father.

"Pardon my asking, but would it be accurate to say that

even after this incident, you still allow your daughter to roam about the streets of Jerusalem unaccompanied?"

Emily didn't like the way this Captain Snodgrass talked over her head. Neither, it seemed, did her father.

"Our home is well guarded, Captain." The major met the other man's challenge. "And we take all the necessary precautions. But Emily has grown up in this city, and I assure you she knows her way around better than you or I."

"And she knows her way around this military facility, as well?"

"Excuse me?" Major Parkinson looked confused. "What are you implying?"

"I'm saying this young lady apparently walked into a secure facility unchallenged, right into this office, in fact. I'm saying you appear to have serious security deficiencies, Major. And my report to Major-General Stockwell will describe them in detail—beginning with your decision to allow your twelve-year-old daughter on critical military operations."

"I'm going on fourteen." Emily felt her face flush.

Captain Snodgrass glared at her.

The young lieutenant looked pale and picked up another piece of her father's pottery, a small vase. He turned it over, frowned, and hummed approvingly.

"You needn't concern yourself about my daughter, Captain." Emily's father clenched his teeth and drummed his fingers on the edge of his desk. "Emily does quite well for herself, and she will be returning home presently. Now, do you have any further questions for her?"

Emily almost felt better at her father's defense, until she realized he must have meant "home" to England, not home to the Rehavia District here in Jerusalem. The understanding dropped to the pit of her stomach.

"I have no further questions for the girl." Captain Snodgrass folded his arms and leaned back in his chair. "But I *do* have several more for you."

Emily didn't need her father to dismiss her. She was out the door and down the hall before anyone could make her cry. And she wished she hadn't understood what had just been said, but she did.

She understood all too well.

"Miss Parkinson!" The young lieutenant ran down the corridor to catch up with her before she left the building. She kept running, but he caught up to her before she could pass through the front door.

"I must apologize on behalf of Captain Snodgrass. He can be a bit, well, abrupt, at times."

"Is that what you call it?" Just then Emily did *not* want to have a conversation, even with the friendly-looking Lieutenant Phipps.

"He means well, Emily." The lieutenant sounded as if he cared. "And he's only concerned about your safety. Just like the rest of us."

Emily nodded but kept her arms crossed, and the handsome young lieutenant rested his hand on her shoulder like a big brother. With his other he pulled a card from his uniform pocket.

"But please, Miss Emily, if you ever feel you need help with anything, will you ring me? This telephone number goes straight through to my desk. Any time."

Emily glanced at the card and read out loud: " 'Lt. Neville Phipps, Special Aide.' " After what had just happened in her father's office with the cranky Captain Ear Wart, it felt good to have a friend. "Thank you."

"I tried to study archaeology at Oxford," he told her, as if she had asked. "Of course, my father had other plans for me. He was an army officer and didn't think digging up old ruins or rummaging around Egyptian pyramids was an honorable profession."

That explained the interest he had shown in her father's old Roman lamp.

"Still," he continued, "antiques are a passion for me. Take that lovely vase in your father's office, for example. A very nice piece—eighteenth-century Italian, I should say." He cleared his throat. "Well, good day, Miss Emily."

"Good day, Lieutenant Phipps. And thanks again."

Emily didn't have the nerve to tell him *she* had made the vase as an art project at the YMCA. She nodded weakly and folded the card into the palm of her hand. "Thank you very much."

BACK-ROOM
TREASURE
5

"You like my treasures?" asked Mr. Bin-Jazzi.

Dov jumped at his voice; he hadn't heard the man sneak up on him. Carefully, he set down the Roman sword next to the dusty table of scrolls—parchments, really.

"I wasn't doing anything wrong." Dov pushed a Roman shield to the side, trying to look as busy as he could. "I was just straightening things up, the way you told me."

Mr. Bin-Jazzi chuckled under his breath as he reached out to pick up the sword. He took a piece of paper from the shelf and dragged it along the blade to easily slice it into ribbons.

"The Romans knew how to make blades. Just be sure this doesn't happen to your fingers."

"I know how to handle a sword." At least, Dov was sure he could figure it out, given a chance.

"Sure, sure." Mr. Bin-Jazzi must have known better. "Don't forget to ask me first, next time."

Dov wasn't sure there would *be* a next time. He wasn't going to stay here in this dusty, dark shop much longer. Two days had been quite enough, thank you. Just long enough to fill his stomach, figure out how to get to the Jewish Quarter, and decide where to search for his family. At the largest synagogue, probably.

"What's the cart for?" Dov picked up his broom and swept a dust storm in the direction of the street. He rooted out a sticky ball of cobwebs from under one of a square wooden cart's bicycle-style wheels. It looked like an oversized wheelbarrow, except for the high wooden sides and the two extra wheels.

"Oh, that." Mr. Bin-Jazzi pushed the cart closer to the wall. "I use it for deliveries, but I tell you, I'm a little tired of pushing it around. Maybe a strong young man like you . . ."

Dov nodded and sneezed but kept up his sweeping while the shopkeeper turned to talk to a customer. Mr. Bin-Jazzi obviously didn't like to throw things away, so Dov decided to help him out. He emptied a couple of small paper sacks filled with old, half-charred scraps of paper. Most were crumpled or rolled into the size of small notes.

Looks like he already tried to burn them once, thought Dov. *I'll finish the job.*

He emptied his own pockets of the lint and dirt he had collected over the past weeks—scraps of paper, assorted garbage—and pushed it all into the pile of burned paper he was shepherding out the door.

But Mr. Bin-Jazzi's face turned pale when he glanced down at Dov's work. "No, no, no, no!" The man moved more quickly than Dov had ever seen before, nearly diving for the pile of rubbish on the floor. "That's not trash!"

Dov held up the broom and wondered what this . . . junk could possibly be, if it wasn't trash.

"I thought—" Dov began.

"Naturally you did." Mr. Bin-Jazzi pulled the note-sized

scraps out one by one, blew on them carefully, and returned them to a shelf. "You had no way of knowing."

"Knowing what?"

Mr. Bin-Jazzi cradled a handful of the paper scraps, which were ripped and yellowed around the edges. For the first time, Dov noticed faded Hebrew writing on one side.

"You had no way of knowing what they are." The old shopkeeper winked at Dov. "But if anyone asks, you tell them they're copies of Zechariah's scrolls."

"Zechariah's . . ." Dov picked one up with two fingers and looked more closely at the faded writing. It *was* Hebrew. Something about *Zion* and *Jerusalem*. He recognized those words right away.

"Copies of the Scriptures. See?" Mr. Bin-Jazzi pointed with his wrinkled finger to the writing. "You're a good Jewish boy. You know the words." The man squinted but didn't seem to need the thick, round glasses resting on the tip of his hawk nose. He knew it by heart. "From the scroll of Zechariah the prophet, chapter eight: 'I am returned unto Zion, and will dwell in the midst of Jerusalem: and Jerusalem shall be called a city of truth; and the mountain of the Lord of hosts the holy mountain.' "

Dov tried to help clean up the scrolls on a squat wooden worktable. But they looked too old to begin with, as if the parchment would crumble in his hands.

"They're not approved by a Jewish scribe or a rabbi, of course." Mr. Bin-Jazzi shook his head. "Can you imagine that, a blessing on Bin-Jazzi's souvenir scrolls? Not only am I an Arab, but a Christian Arab, at that." He laughed loudly. "A double blessing the rabbis may not appreciate as much as I!"

"Where did you find them?" Dov lowered his voice, and

the shopkeeper laughed again. Dov wasn't sure what was so funny.

"I made them myself! Don't you see? They're copies, not real scrolls. I sell them to pilgrims and tourists. Most of them wouldn't know *aleph* from *zayin, a* from *z.*"

Dov was glad he did.

"Still, they buy them. Souvenirs from the Holy Land."

"Souvenirs . . ." echoed Dov. The back room was full of them.

"Yes, and you be sure to tell customers just that. Farouk Bin-Jazzi is an honest shopkeeper! And we sell souvenirs, not real artifacts—although the words on them are very real."

Dov nodded. Fine. The man had a right to sell whatever he wanted to, including new parchments made to look old. What did Dov care?

"The Old City is filled with such things." Mr. Bin-Jazzi dismissed Dov with a wave of his hand. "Maybe because we're built upon layer after layer of history, hundreds of feet deep. Jews, Romans, Byzantines, Muslims, Crusaders . . . Do you know how many cities lie below your feet, how many people have lived on these hills, for thousands of years?"

Dov shook his head. "They probably all stored their old things in this room, though."

Mr. Bin-Jazzi laughed and pointed behind the table, toward a stack of wooden crates piled nearly to the ceiling, next to the collection of olive-wood branches, next to the pile of slightly broken pottery, next to . . .

"There's a trapdoor in the floor under there somewhere. But I tell you so you stay away, not so you'll look for it."

"Trapdoor?" Dov's ears perked up.

"To the cisterns."

"Cisterns?"

"Yes, you know—big stone pits for storing rainwater."

"Is that where you get your drinking water?"

"No, no." Mr. Bin-Jazzi chuckled. "They haven't been used since the Roman times. King Herod built them more than two thousand years ago for the temple. But I suppose if they weren't filled in with rubble, they'd be just large enough to give my elephant a bath."

Dov had to think for a moment before he realized Mr. Bin-Jazzi had to be joking about the elephant.

"How many are there?"

"I have no idea. Five. Ten. Twenty. I understand they're connected by tunnels. Or were."

Mr. Bin-Jazzi dropped the last comment as if he were chatting about the weather. As if secret tunnels under the floor were nothing to worry about.

"Tunnels," Dov whispered. "Under the Temple Mount."

"I didn't say that, exactly." Mr. Bin-Jazzi shook his head. "No one knows how far the cisterns go. But my Muslim neighbors wouldn't like hearing about secret tunnels that opened into the home of an infidel like me. Especially not if the tunnels led under their *Haram es-Sharif.*"

He meant the famous Dome of the Rock that had been built over the top of the Jewish temple ruins. The tall dome shrine on all the picture postcards of the city.

"Why the door?" Dov still wanted to know.

"Ah yes, the door. Well, I suppose a few of the cisterns were not filled in completely, so my father used to store food in them. It's cool and dark down there. But this was years ago, when I was still a young man."

"So you've been down there?"

"Never. And don't get any ideas." He wagged his finger in Dov's face so there was no mistaking the warning. "Rats the size of dogs live in those cisterns."

Rats, with sharp teeth. Dov shivered as he lifted his shoe and looked down at the well-worn blue-patterned tiles. Rats reminded him of the labor camps.

And that was not a memory he wanted to hold on to.

Dov would have listened to Mr. Bin-Jazzi's stories all afternoon if someone had not entered the shop. The shopkeeper picked up one last scrap of paper from the floor and was about to toss it aside when he stopped.

"Emily Parkinson?" It was his turn to look puzzled as he read the note. " 'One-twenty-three Ezra Road'? That's a fine neighborhood. But I thought all the British had left."

Dov wasn't sure what the man was talking about; he had seen plenty of British soldiers since he'd arrived in the city. Instead of trying to explain, he snatched the small piece of ripped paper from Mr. Bin-Jazzi's hand.

The man grinned. "Your girlfriend's address, is that it?"

"Girlfriend?" Dov sputtered. "No!"

He hadn't noticed the tiny letters on the back of the paper when he'd wadded it up and tossed it in the trash pile a few minutes earlier. That Emily Parkinson! She must have slipped the address into his pocket while they were riding together in the American car on their way here to Jerusalem a few days ago. But why?

I should have ripped the note into a thousand pieces.

Or maybe not. Who else did he know in this strange place? He shoved the note back into his pocket and once again attacked the dust with his broom. He could always throw it away later. Thankfully, Mr. Bin-Jazzi didn't say anything else, just chuckled and returned to the front room to greet his customer.

A moment later a dozen Arabic voices seemed to talk at

once, but even Dov could tell they were not haggling over the price of a watermelon. There was Mr. Bin-Jazzi's voice, too, in the middle of the angry exchange. But where the others were sharp and tense, the shopkeeper met the challengers with calm, steady words. Dov inched forward quietly. He had to see what was going on.

"*Ghabee!*" sneered one of the visitors.

When Dov finally peeked around the red curtain in the doorway between the two rooms, he saw Mr. Bin-Jazzi backed into the corner near the spices. The shopkeeper held up his hands for peace and answered back in a low voice.

Obviously it wasn't enough to satisfy the other man, a much younger fellow with a dark mustache and wearing a dirty khaki shirt and black slacks. The intruder's traditional white kaffiyeh bobbed about on his head every time he waved his angry hands. Behind him, three other thugs had also crowded into the shop. One guarded the door; the other two lined up behind the man in the khaki shirt.

For just a moment, Dov clenched his fist. *How dare they do this?*

He even thought of pulling the curtain aside and telling these bullies . . . But no. Dov watched quietly. This was not his fight.

The shopkeeper probably has it coming. And besides, it's none of my business. None at all.

Still, Dov couldn't help but be impressed by the ice-cool Mr. Bin-Jazzi, as if the man had become the peaceful eye of a sudden and very violent storm.

And Dov needed no one to translate: Mr. Khaki's sharp finger an inch from Mr. Bin-Jazzi's nose spoke a language anyone could understand.

You listen to me.

Mr. Bin-Jazzi could not back up any more as he sat back into an open barrel of saffron. Why was no one coming to his rescue? Dov wondered. Surely people could hear the ruckus from out on the street.

Of course, there was the guard by the door who cradled an ancient hunting rifle in the folds of his white robe. Dov realized anyone passing by on the street would be able to see the man's silent warning.

Stay out of this shop.

The visitors' shouting became louder, and Mr. Khaki shoved Mr. Bin-Jazzi in the chest, knocking over the barrels of saffron and allspice and sending him crashing to the floor.

Even so, Dov stood statue-still behind the curtain, doing his best not to sneeze at the cloud of spices that filled the air. His eyes watered; his stomach flipped. He held a hand over his nose and mouth, but it was too late.

With a grunt, he did his best to stifle a sneeze that would have been heard all the way into the New City.

THREAD OF HOPE

Emily paused a moment before pushing the office door open. She pretended to fix her hair with her hand as she peeked at her reflection in the window of the Jewish Agency office. Behind her, the usual Thursday-afternoon crowds on King George Avenue hurried by.

No one will know who I am, she told herself, and it was probably true. She had never visited the Search Bureau for Missing Relatives before. She hardly ever had any reason to visit this part of Jerusalem. So they would never know she was Emily Parkinson, daughter of Major Alan Parkinson, Eighty-seventh Airborne Regiment.

If I don't try, I'll never know.

That was enough to convince herself. She needed to know, but not because she was curious. Just because.

And what if I find them?

She would decide what to do then. Almost surely these people would have no idea where Dov's family was, just like at her father's office. She looked behind her once more, just to be sure, and pushed her way inside.

Good. Five minutes and I'll be gone.

At least, that was the idea. But five minutes turned to ten, and ten to thirty. The line that snaked its way through the office proved longer than Emily had hoped—much longer.

Actually, after a half hour the line had shortened to about twenty people in front of her. Most stared straight ahead and wore grim, hopeless expressions. Many wore equally grim, threadless shirts or sweaters with the elbows worn away—worse than what Emily's mother threw in the rubbish or saved for the Ruth Sewing Circle annual charity drive at Saint Andrew's Church.

And speaking of her parents, Emily was quite glad her father hadn't been around the house that afternoon to see her go. If this line stretched out much longer, her parents were going to start wondering if Emily had been kidnapped again.

Especially when she had told the guard by their front door that she was going out for a short walk. *Short?* Well, yes, it was, as a matter of fact. They moved slowly down the hall, a half step every few minutes. At this rate it certainly wasn't a *long* walk.

"Beautiful weather outside, don't you think?" After forty-five minutes Emily finally got up the courage to say something to the blank-faced woman behind her. But it took a moment or two for the woman to respond.

"Did you say something?" The woman straightened her plain white blouse and looked around as if for the first time.

She had been pretty once, Emily could tell. But today worry lines streaked her face, and she wiped away a tear.

"It was nothing." Emily used her best Hebrew, hoping no one could tell the difference. Their gardener, Mr. Liebermann, had once told her she spoke like a *sabra*. A native. Someone who had been born in Palestine.

The woman with the worried face nodded and returned to whatever faraway place her thoughts had taken her. Somewhere happier, Emily guessed, with someone she loved, now lost. For a moment Emily thought of trying to say something else, but she could tell there was no open door into this woman's world.

And so she kept quiet as the line shuffled on. Another half hour later it was finally her turn, and she stood in front of three desks at the far end of the office. A young woman with tired gray eyes waved her over.

"This way. Come on. Next."

The woman's battered steel army desk looked as if it had been dropped out of a plane without a parachute. Emily was afraid to speak very loudly, for fear her breath would topple the stacks of onionskin paper on each corner, each piled at least as high as the tired woman's starched black hair.

"Speak up, would you?" The woman looked through Emily as if she were a pane of glass. Or perhaps just a pain, with fifty more impossible problems and sad stories behind her.

"I, uh . . ." Emily eyed the stacks of paper once more. "I'm here to find out about . . ."

And so she launched into her story. Or Dov's story, actually, about the Zalinski family of Warsaw. She did her best to remember all the details Dov had told her about his family's plans to come to Palestine.

"These are your people, these Zalinskis?"

Emily remembered the same questions back at her father's office and shook her head.

"Hmm. Zalinski." The clerk repeated the name over and over as she thumbed through one of the stacks in front of her.

Emily was ready to jump away if it toppled. But there was

no need; the clerk must have done this before. With a sweep of her hand, she snapped a paper from the bottom of the pile. Somehow the onionskin didn't rip.

"Friends of your family, then?"

Again Emily shook her head. "Not exactly."

The clerk squinted up at Emily, obviously waiting for a reason to continue her search.

"Did you find them?" Emily held her breath.

The woman scanned her report, shook her head, and replaced the paper.

"No. Not here."

Oh well. Emily sighed. *What's the worst that could happen if I mention Daddy's name?*

"My father is Major Parkinson," Emily finally admitted. Maybe it would help. And for a moment, Emily thought it had.

The clerk raised her eyebrows, stared at Emily, and immediately switched over to English. "Well, then, Miss Parkinson. You can tell the major that I have no records of this Mordecai Zalinski from Warsaw, either. Unless, of course, you care to look through some of the past records yourself." The woman pointed at a wall stacked high with worn black binders, each stuffed with dog-eared forms.

Emily sighed. How many years would this search take? And why exactly was she doing this? She wasn't sure.

"Perhaps I can come back sometime?" Emily took a half step back from the desk.

"Don't bother." The woman held up her hand as if to signal the next person in line, then looked at Emily and sighed. "Oh, all right. If you promise to stop bothering me, I'll put in a request for your information, all right? I know who your father is."

Emily smiled and nodded. "Thank you, miss, I—"

"Next." There would be no more small talk. The clerk once again looked through Emily to see who was next in line. She motioned to the woman with the worried face to step forward, and Emily shuffled slowly back out of the room.

That was a waste, she told herself, but as she left the office she picked up a familiar, well-read newspaper from a chair in the front waiting room—the *Palestine Gazette,* published in English by the British government. Her father always brought it home from work, and until then she'd thought it was only good for lining the bottom of the kitchen garbage can under the sink.

But not this time, she thought as she studied one of the tattered pages and stepped back out into the late-afternoon sunshine still bathing King George Avenue. The autumn air seemed thinner, nippier, and it rustled the page into her face. She slapped it back flat.

" 'Public Notice,' " she read quietly, stepping away from an older woman walking a little hairless dog. " 'The following name changes have been registered at the office of the commissioner for migration and statistics.' "

Normally that would have been enough to easily put her to sleep. But look here: a list of people who had come to Palestine and changed their names!

Emily knew it often happened. Jews by the thousands coming from Europe didn't want to keep their old German, Hungarian, or Polish names. Perhaps it reminded them of their past, the one they all wanted to forget. In any case, many applied for new Jewish names in their new country. She ran her finger down the long list from the column marked *Old Name* to the one marked *New Name.*

Old Name: Elia Dimentshtein. New Name: Eliyahu Ben-

Tsevi. That certainly sounded Jewish enough.

Old Name: Ora Sonnenshein. New Name: Ora Shamir. At least she kept her first name. And down the list, to the bottom of the third page, to the names that began in *T, U, V . . .* finally *Z.*

The hairless dog on the sidewalk next to her tripped at Emily's ankle, tangling the leather leash while its owner crowed a complaint. But Emily hardly noticed. Because there it was.

Old Name: Natan Zalinski. New Name: Natan Israeli. Nationality: Palestinian (which could have meant Arab or Jew, either one). *Address: Tel Aviv.*

"Excuse me." The woman with the dog pointed at Emily's feet.

Emily looked down to find the leash completely wrapped around her ankles. She lifted her feet, lost one of her brown shoes on the sidewalk, and had to skip to keep from falling on her face.

But he has the wrong first name! Emily studied the newspaper for more clues. She found none. It was *Natan* Zalinski, and she had no idea who that might be. It certainly wasn't a name she'd heard from Dov, and probably not worth getting excited about. Perhaps it was a relative of some kind, but she had no way of telling. Besides, she had no real desire to learn all about the Jewish boy's family tree. None, in fact. Interesting, though, how the person had changed *Zalinski* to *Israeli.*

"Come, Bruno!" The woman gathered her rat-sized dog and hurried down the street—as if Emily had in some way offended her by scaring Bruno.

Emily sighed, stepped back into her shoe, and stuffed the

newspaper into her green canvas backpack.

She would have to keep looking.

But what was the chance of finding anyone? And why did it matter so much to her?

INFIDEL!

7

Dov sneezed again and again as the horrible, burning sweet scent of Mr. Bin-Jazzi's spices filled the air of the shop like a yellow fog. The curtain he hid behind did nothing to hold it back, just as he could not hold back his own tears. When he tried to plug his nose, the pressure only grew worse and worse; he blew out his ears.

All that was left now was for the intruders to yank the curtain away from his hiding place and drag Dov out like a dog. If they did, though, Dov would make the men regret it. Through his watering eyes, Dov looked around the dark back room for something to defend himself with. His broom was better than nothing, and he stood ready, shaking, gripping the broomstick with white knuckles.

Only no one came.

Instead, the men in the front room just shouted and sneezed and spat and cursed. Loudly enough, Dov supposed, that they might not have heard his own sneezing fit. He closed his eyes for a moment and breathed a sigh of relief but jumped when he heard pottery shattering on the hard stone floor. Some of Mr. Bin-Jazzi's precious antiquities?

He heard more smashing, more snarling and complaining from the men. Through it all, Dov heard one voice over the others. Not that it was louder—no, just the opposite. Mr. Bin-Jazzi still managed to sound different. It wasn't more than a minute or two before Dov realized the angry voices, the other voices, had finally left.

Still Mr. Bin-Jazzi continued, almost singing, then whispering, then softer still. Talking to himself? Dov found the courage to peek around the edge of the red curtain.

"Are you all right?" It was a silly question, Dov knew. Mr. Bin-Jazzi would not be all right after the scuffle Dov had heard. Dov recognized the men from the street as the kind who would leave behind bruises and threats.

Mr. Bin-Jazzi was still on the floor, on his knees in the middle of the mess of spices. The cloud had settled, but it still tickled Dov's nose, and he had to sneeze once more.

The shopkeeper didn't turn, didn't stop his mumbling, only changed from Arabic to English without seeming to miss a word.

"And, my Lord," said Mr. Bin-Jazzi, his voice low and breaking, "the same as you have reached down to me . . ."

He's praying. Dov took a step backward, as if he were about to step on a snake. He didn't quite know what to do with knowing the prayer was meant for his ears, too.

" . . . and allowed me to be your child through faith in *Isa al-Masih*, please reach down to the lives of those men, as well as the young harami, the thief you have sent to help me. Forgive them, as I do."

"I'm not a . . ." Dov began to protest, but of course he was exactly what Mr. Bin-Jazzi had called him.

Harami. Thief. Yet Dov wasn't so sure about being sent

by God. He frowned and tried to clear his mind.

I have to get out of this crazy place, he told himself as he tried to slip past the kneeling man. *Right now!*

He tiptoed past the upturned barrels, the broken pottery shards, the spices all over the floor. Just three or four steps to the doorway, and he would be free. . . .

"Amen." The man finally rose to his feet after making the sign of the cross on his chest and forehead. Up, down, left, right. Dov had seen Christians do that before.

"I'm glad you stayed in the back room," said Mr. Bin-Jazzi. "Although I don't know how they didn't hear you sneezing." The edge of his mouth turned up in a tiny grin. "God was watching out for us."

"How can you say that?" Dov looked around at the ruined shop. "Can't you see what a mess—"

Dov slipped in a dry puddle of peppercorns when he took another step toward the door. The only place to reach for help was Mr. Bin-Jazzi's square shoulders.

"Watch yourself, now." The man gripped Dov's elbows and held on, even after Dov found his footing again. Dov tried to get away, but Mr. Bin-Jazzi would not let go.

"Now, you were wondering whether God was watching out for us? Do you doubt that it is so?"

"I don't know." Dov wished his legs would move. They felt like rubber. "Let me go."

Mr. Bin-Jazzi let go and stepped back carefully, but now his stare kept Dov from running.

"I know that you have probably seen things a young child should never see. I have read about the war, heard things. I'm sorry."

Dov studied the floor. This was not a conversation he cared to have.

Even so, the man went on. "But you think I'm a stranger to sadness? Look around you. What do you see?"

Dov sighed and pressed his lips together.

Mr. Bin-Jazzi stared at him with tears in his eyes. "You see a wife and children?" He swept his arm around. "Grandchildren? Where are they? You've been under my roof for three nights, and you have not asked?"

Somehow it hadn't occurred to Dov that the man had no family. He'd just been thinking about his own.

Mr. Bin-Jazzi stared out the open door of his shop, and his eyes seemed far, far away. "Then I'll tell you anyway. Twenty-five years ago—this is 1922, eh? When I was a younger man, and stronger, I had a wife and a young son. Our son, little Rudah . . . I was so proud. Did I tell you this was 1922? Well, that was the year the influenza came to our neighborhood."

Dov had a sinking feeling now that he knew what would come next.

"They died." Tears still filled the man's eyes, but he did not wipe them away. "She and our young son, both. And me . . . I could only watch."

Dov looked in the same direction, as if that would help him see the past, as well. Not that he wanted to see, but for just a moment, he felt a stab of pain for the man. And for just a moment, he thought he might know how Mr. Bin-Jazzi felt.

"I didn't know . . ." The words slipped from Dov's tongue.

"It was a long time ago." Mr. Bin-Jazzi took a deep breath and looked around his shop. "Long before you were born. And I tell you only so you understand."

Understand what?

" 'Though he slay me, yet will I trust in him,' isn't that right?"

Mr. Bin-Jazzi must have seen the confused look on Dov's face.

"Another Bible verse, my Jewish friend." He patted Dov on the back. "The book of Job, if I remember correctly. Now, let's get this cleaned up, so we can see about finding *your* family."

Dov stood his ground, wondering if he still had a chance of getting away, or if he still wanted to.

"Well?" Mr. Bin-Jazzi picked up the broom Dov had dropped on the floor and held it out to him.

"But what about—"

"Oh, *them*?" The shopkeeper waved at the doorway as if he were shooing a fly. "I've run into Atallah and those other young men before. They're angry at everyone. And they call themselves patriots, *watani*. I call them common criminals, and not very smart ones, at that."

"But why did they attack you?"

"It's none of your concern," the man finally answered, casually stroking his chin as if they were talking about the weather. "But in case they come back, perhaps you should know they want me to store their dirty guns in my back room for them."

"And they don't have their own back rooms?"

At that, Mr. Bin-Jazzi leaned his head back and laughed. "I asked them the exact same question, my young friend. That's when they got even nastier. But I already knew the answer. They think the police will never think to look here. And if they ever *did*, who would get the blame?"

Dov's eyes widened as the shopkeeper told his story.

"Perhaps they're right about the police. I have a good reputation. But no guns, I tell them. Never! So that made them . . . a little upset."

"A *little* upset?"

"All right." Mr. Bin-Jazzi shrugged. "Spitting mad. But still that won't change anything. I live here on the Street of the Chain, and I will die here. Just like my father, and his father before him. And I will continue to forgive them and pray for them." He grinned. "*That's* what really makes them mad, I'm thinking."

Dov could only shake his head.

"And what would *you* do if you were me, Mr. Dov Zalinski?"

"I would not pray for *them*."

Mr. Bin-Jazzi chuckled softly. "Our Scriptures say that 'whosoever hateth his brother is a murderer,' do they not?" He thumped his chest. "Farouk Bin-Jazzi is no murderer!"

"But they are no brothers."

"That's where you're wrong, my friend. You stay here with me, and you will learn."

Mr. Bin-Jazzi patted Dov on the shoulder before he left the room, and the warm glow in his brown eyes almost convinced Dov to smile back.

Almost.

Instead, Dov shrugged and went back to his sweeping.

He's just like Henrik, the way he talks.

Just like Henrik, the Danish Jew at Kibbutz Yad Shalom, where Dov had spent his first days in Palestine. Forgive your enemies? How could he?

Fine. Thugs can break in and destroy this place, I'll sweep up the mess, and Mr. Bin-Jazzi can say 'I forgive you' all he wants. If that's what he wants to do, that's his business.

Still, Dov couldn't shake the odd feeling that Henrik and Mr. Bin-Jazzi knew something he didn't. Had he stumbled onto the stage of a play, where he was the only one who didn't know his lines? First it was Henrik and his stepfather, Matthias, the Swedish Red Cross worker he'd met on the refugee ship. And now Farouk Bin-Jazzi, this crazy Arab Christian who prayed for his enemies only seconds after they had pushed him around in his own shop!

Were they all reading from the same script—a script Dov didn't have?

Or maybe the spices in the air had just gone to the man's head. Yes, that had to be it. Dov tried to plug his nose as he swept some more.

One more meal, and he would be gone.

Five weeks later, Dov followed Mr. Bin-Jazzi down the crowded street, clutching the small cloth sack with the good Arabic-style food the shopkeeper had prepared for him. He could still feel the warmth from the flat pita bread shells of his two *falafels*, and he had to smile.

"What's this?" he had asked Mr. Bin-Jazzi the first time he tried one. The shopkeeper had shown him how to eat the Arab delicacy, and he had to admit it wasn't bad. In fact, the chick-pea stuffing tasted a lot like meatballs, and meatballs were something Dov had eaten only once or twice in his entire life.

Not that he hadn't worked for his meals—worked hard. Mr. Bin-Jazzi saw to that. Besides the cleanup, Dov served as a human mule, pushing that old delivery cart through the crowded streets with the strange names: Street of the Chain, of course, Ha Shal-shelet. But also up and down the busy *El-Wad* to the Damascus Gate. Or the street called *El-Khaldiya*, or even into the narrow and smoky covered *Suq el-Kattanin*.

He didn't particularly like it in there—the "Sook" seemed more like a cave than a market street.

The men in the doorways or cooking their suppers over small charcoal fires always recognized the cart. "Where are you going?" they would all ask. And he didn't usually have Mr. Bin-Jazzi to answer for him, the way he did today. So he just did a lot of smiling and waving.

Now it was Mr. Bin-Jazzi's turn to smile and wave to the people they passed, though Dov noticed not too many smiled back. Just behind their waving hands, Dov thought he could see the frown, hear the whispered threat.

Kafir.

That had been the first Arabic word Dov had learned after Atallah and the other toughs came in to break up the shop. A little boy had run past the shop with a stick, hitting the walls and shouting for the whole neighborhood to hear, "Kafir! Kafir!"

"So we begin your lessons in Arabic with a name they call me," Mr. Bin-Jazzi had told him with a hint of a grin on his face. " 'Kafir' means 'infidel,' someone who has turned away from the faith. But of course I have not; I hold to the faith of my father and his fathers before him, all the way back to Isa al-Masih, the Lord Jesus himself! Infidel? Ha! It is *they* who . . ."

And then he had stopped himself, turned away, and made the sign of the cross once more on his forehead and chest. He had mumbled something Dov didn't quite understand about how his friend Father Samuel had warned him against pride.

Pride? Dov had never heard anyone talk about such things. Surely this kind man could not be guilty of very much. Every day, Dov found himself learning more, though he had promised himself he would not. Mr. Bin-Jazzi ordered him around like an army sergeant, but he always made sure Dov had enough to eat. And he was always trying to teach him new Arabic words.

Sabah al-khayr. Good morning.

Shukran. Thank you.

Salaam. Peace.

Of course, there was precious little salaam in Mr. Bin-Jazzi's neighborhood. Dov wondered if the Arab gang would return, but the shopkeeper would not speak of it. Even so, he had admitted that things were getting worse in Jerusalem. Every day they watched more and more British soldiers passing by their shop door in nervous groups of four, six, or eight soldiers. Their ugly gray rifles were always drawn, and their fingers rested on the triggers. Mr. Bin-Jazzi seemed to hold his breath every time they went by.

"What do they want?" Dov had wondered aloud. "Why don't they go home?"

Mr. Bin-Jazzi always had the same reply for him. Something about "Is it not written?" or "In this world ye shall have tribulation: but be of good cheer; I have overcome the world." He was talking about the Messiah, of course, or as Mr. Bin-Jazzi preferred to call Him, Isa al-Masih. He talked endlessly about Isa al-Masih. There was no shortage of lessons in Mr. Farouk Bin-Jazzi's Golden Rock Factory for Olive Wood.

Even now, as they threaded their way past a barbershop toward where a Jewish street would dead-end at Ha Shalshelet, the lessons continued.

"Promise me you'll be careful." Mr. Bin-Jazzi whispered the words over his shoulder, and Dov had to nearly step on the man's heels to hear. "*Hather.* 'Careful.'"

"*Insha'allah.*" Yes, if God wills it. He had learned that much. They had talked over their plan now a dozen times.

"You'll come back to see me after you've found your parents, yes?"

Dov nodded; he could not say no. Not after what Mr. Bin-Jazzi had done for him. He patted the gift in his pocket—the special treat Mr. Bin-Jazzi had prepared. *Teen mutabra*, figs dried with anise seed and wrapped in a white handkerchief. To eat later, Mr. Bin-Jazzi had told him.

"Directly down this street, *Hayehudim*, then the Hurva Synagogue will be on your left. Someone there will help you. Don't worry."

Dov knew Mr. Bin-Jazzi was right. So why did he suddenly want to run back to the shop to eat just one more meal with him?

"Go," said Mr. Bin-Jazzi. "It is time."

Dov crossed over to the other side of the street, as he had been told. He tried not to look at the two British guards who blocked his way from the Muslim neighborhood to the Jewish neighborhood. Only a matter of feet, and the world changed.

"You there, young man!" cried a guard.

Dov's heart raced, but he reminded himself Mr. Bin-Jazzi would be speaking to the British, not he.

That was the plan, Dov's chance to slip through—a second or two when the officers were distracted by Mr. Bin-Jazzi.

But Dov paused for just a moment when the older man started coughing, waving for help.

That wasn't part of the plan!

Or was it? But by this time Mr. Bin-Jazzi was doubled over, nearly falling on the street. He was either a wonderful actor, or . . . Dov couldn't wonder, couldn't wait. He brushed by the soldiers and slipped through the narrow entry to Hayehudim Street, put his head down, and ran.

"Hold it!" yelled another soldier.

Too late. Dov had covered nearly a half block before he dared look back. Back at the checkpoint, the soldiers were still helping Mr. Bin-Jazzi to his feet. Dov thought he caught his eye; he couldn't be sure.

"I'll be back," Dov promised—just before he felt a large hand clamp down on his shoulder.

THE GABBAI HELPS

8

"You would be lost, young man?"

The hand had a voice, and the voice belonged to a hollow-cheeked man in a black suit, a black hat, and matching black beard. *One of the Orthodox!* He didn't smile, but his voice was kind.

"Yes . . . I mean, no!" Dov finally found his own voice, the stiff Hebrew he had learned as a child. He would have been most comfortable in Yiddish, but he was afraid to try anything different. What if the people here in the Jewish Quarter of the Old City spoke only Hebrew?

"Then who is your father?" The man quizzed him as if he were an unofficial gatekeeper.

"My father . . ." Dov's mind raced at the question, and he wished he could remember more. "His name is Mordecai Zalinski. From Warsaw."

"And what makes you think your father would come all the way from Warsaw to this neighborhood?"

Dov held up his hands and shook his head. "He always said *'iber a yor—'*"

"Iber a yor in Yerushalayim," interrupted the man, speaking the words Dov had known when he was little. " 'Next year in Jerusalem.' Yes, of course he did, just as every other Jew in the world. You still didn't answer my question."

Dov knew he probably couldn't.

"I was going to the Hurva Synagogue," he finally told the man. "Mr. Farouk Bin-Jazzi said—"

"Who?" The man's eyes narrowed when Dov mentioned the Arab name.

"Oh. I mean, someone told me it's the biggest synagogue in the Old City and perhaps someone there would be able to help me. I was hoping maybe they could tell me if they've seen Abba or Imma. Or Natan."

The man shook his head and frowned. "Everybody is looking for someone these days. Ever since the end of the war. That's why we have the Search Bureau for Missing Relatives."

He paused for a moment, then sighed and rolled his eyes.

"All right, then. You come with me. You can speak with the *gabbai*. But if I were you, I wouldn't mention to anyone that you came in from the Muslim Quarter."

Dov nodded at the warning and followed his new host. He wasn't sure he remembered what a gabbai was, but he supposed he would find out soon enough.

Soon enough turned into an hour after he had met the man in the black suit. Considering where he stood, though, he was content waiting quietly to see the gabbai.

"Beautiful," Dov said in a hushed voice, and the words seemed to carry all the way up to the high dome ceiling of the Hurva Synagogue. All the way up and back. It was as if anything he said in this magnificent room turned into a prayer. The inside of the dome was painted a deep sky-blue and was studded with painted gold stars; Dov supposed he had never seen such an amazing building before in his life.

Beautiful, from the row upon row of fine carved wooden benches to the sparkling crystal chandeliers overhead, and back down to the platform in the middle. The air carried a faint hint of dark, carved mahogany and cool stone, of candles waiting to be lit for the next service. And from the west, toward the New City, a ray of afternoon sunlight splintered into a thousand colors where it filtered through stained-glass windows. Dov wasn't sure what the symbols in the windows meant, but they were beautiful, too, and so were the commanding walls all around him, straight and proud.

"Is this where you live, God?" he whispered. "Can you hear me? Because if you can, then I wish you'd show me how to find my family."

Only the silence echoed around him.

"Because if you can, then I wish you'd show me how to find my family."

Suddenly he felt silly. He crossed his arms and turned slowly around, trying to take it all in. At first looking made him dizzy, but he could not stop until he noticed a red beam of light spotlighting the *aron kodesh* perched on a shelf along the eastern wall.

The aron kodesh, the *holy ark*—a fancy wooden covering for the scrolls—looked to be more than half his height, finely carved and carefully overlaid with glittering gold-leaf swirls. It would take a strong man or two to carry it, and then very carefully, indeed. As Dov stared at the ark, it almost reminded him of a giant wooden cocoon, or maybe a small case for a mummy.

No, not a mummy case. Most certainly not. He chased that thought out of his mind as quickly as it had entered, for it seemed disrespectful in a place like this. Dov felt as if God himself were listening closely to his thoughts here. And perhaps He was.

In a place like the Hurva Synagogue, Dov was sure he was seeing a proper aron kodesh, with a proper scroll inside, written by a proper scribe. Nothing like Mr. Bin-Jazzi's tourist scrolls, of course. At least he knew *that* much about synagogues. The scroll he remembered from back home in Warsaw was smaller, not quite as grand. He couldn't recall much about it, though he did remember it had been covered by a fine maroon embroidered cloth, much like the one draped over the top of this one. There had been a name for such a cloth, too, thought Dov, but he could not remember *that*, either. But everything in a synagogue had a name, a purpose, a meaning.

He stood there in the cool hush, trying his best to fish long-forgotten memories from the back of his mind. Memories of going with his father to *Shabbat* services on Friday evening, walking down Gensia Street to the corner, past the butcher who hung kosher sausages in his window. Coming to a place like this, only smaller, and filled with people. And . . .

"Oh, *there* you are."

A voice behind Dov made him jump. His memories evaporated into the stones of the Hurva, and he squinted at the bright light of a door behind him. A straight-backed man hurried toward him, his heels clicking on the ivory marble floor.

"You shouldn't be in here just now." The man spoke in rapid-fire bursts of air. "Come with me."

"Are you the—"

"I'm the gabbai, yes. My name is Mendel. I take care of

business here at the synagogue."

"I didn't know. I—"

"Yes, I'm sure you didn't." He paused at the door where he had come in. "But it *is* a beautiful place, isn't it?"

Dov almost had to run to keep up with Mendel, the gabbai. Not to be confused with the *rabbi*, of course. He followed him down a side hall to a small meeting room of some sort. At the same time, men were just coming in from the street. While Dov stood there, Mendel quietly mumbled a few words to the others.

No one asked Dov to sit down, but at least he had their attention.

"You came here because. . . ?" one of the bearded men wanted to know.

They all looked very much alike in their black coats and hats. Many had gray hair and beards. Most had draped white prayer shawls over their shoulders, the kind with tassels and blue stripes. Maybe it would be time to pray soon, though Dov wasn't sure he should stay for that. He had already prayed back in the domed sanctuary.

He explained about his parents, told them his family name and how he knew they would be looking for him, too. They would have come here to this synagogue because . . .

"I'm sorry, but we have no Zalinskis here." The oldest-looking man rested on his twisted cane as he looked around at the rest of the group. Everyone else shook their heads. "There's Berzovski. Godlewski. Kitegorodski."

"But no Zalinski?"

"No Zalinski." The man tugged at his beard. "From Warsaw, you say?"

Dov nodded.

"I had a cousin from Warsaw," said one of the other men. "He died in forty-four."

The men spent the next ten minutes remembering all their friends and relatives who had died, then friends of relatives, and then relatives of friends. Samuel Feldman and his wife, Sarah. Yehuda Mendelbaum. Daniel and Devora Cohen . . .

"So you've never heard of my family?" Dov thought he would try once more, just in case.

Each looked to the oldest man with their sad, sunken eyes, as if he was the only one who could break the news.

"Listen, son. Do you know how many have come here to Eretz Israel, the only survivors of their families?"

Dov knew what was coming next. He balled his fists and held his breath as the man went on.

"Do you know how many were killed? Fathers and mothers, all gone. Hitler and his—"

"NO!" Dov's protest dropped the jaws of every man in the room. But Dov didn't care. "I don't want to hear it anymore!"

What did they know? Nothing. He was wasting his time here. He started for the door.

"Now, wait a minute, boy," said the old man. "We're just trying to explain."

But Dov couldn't turn around, or they would see his face. He wiped a hot tear away with the sleeve of his shirt and paused at the door. "Everyone always talks about all the dead people. Well, I'm *alive*, and so are my parents."

"Now, hold on," one of the men began. "You'd better face up to the truth."

"I don't care what you say. I'm going to find them."

With that, he pushed open the door to the street but came

face-to-face with a latecomer. No matter. Dov stepped to the side and hurried down the narrow way with his hands jammed into his pockets.

They can say their prayers all day, for all I care, there inside their safe walls. But do they know anything important? Do they know where Abba and Imma are?

He would have kept walking if he'd known which way to walk. He blocked out the sights and sounds of the people around him. But even when he clamped his hands over his ears, he could not escape the echoes of the men's words.

"You'd better face up to the truth."

He thought he *had*. That's why he was here in Jerusalem, right?

"Face up to the truth."

But Imma had promised they'd meet again. Even if that was all Dov could remember of her, he remembered the promise.

". . . to the truth."

Dov's eyes stung, and the voices followed him. But there—a dark doorway leading to a covered alley would give him a place to rest. He hung his head and tried to stop the tears.

He couldn't.

"You have a lot to learn, young fellow."

Dov didn't look up, but he recognized the gabbai's voice. Gabbai Mendel. What did *he* want?

"You don't speak to those men like that. Do you hear what I'm saying?"

Dov nodded without turning. Another lecture?

"If it makes you feel any better, I lost most of my family, too. A lot of us did. That's what they were trying to tell you."

This time Dov was too tired to feel angry. All he could do

was nod and sniffle like a baby. The gabbai kept talking.

"All right, you want some advice?"

Dov closed his eyes. "I'm listening."

"Do you know where the Yemin Moshe neighborhood is?"

Dov nodded his head. He had heard of it before. . . .

"Out Zion Gate, to the right, past Mount Zion on the left and the big Church of the Dormition."

Dov nodded again. He thought he remembered something about a Zion Gate, too.

". . . then straight across the Hinnom Valley to a gateway with a Star of David in the arch. The home you're seeking is on the hill just above that. In the place called Yemin Moshe, under the windmill."

"Why are you telling me this?"

"Just listen. Go to the back door of the house on Number 3 Malki Street quietly, understand? Over the fence, through the garden in back. *Not* the front door."

"Why not?"

"No questions. The people there might be able to help you. She's American—Jewish. He's British, but he's all right. They're *Haganah*. Do you know what that is?"

This time Dov nodded more quickly. He'd heard of Haganah before. The Jewish secret forces.

"And if they ask, tell them their friend the gabbai sent you."

"I thought you said your name was Mendel."

"The name isn't important. What's important is that you keep quiet about what I just told you. Just do it. Now, can you remember all that?"

"I'll remember. Thank—" Dov swallowed hard, wiped his nose on his shirt sleeve, and turned around.

The gabbai was gone.

WHAT IF I STAYED?

9

"Down, Julian." Emily tried to push her family's Great Dane away, but he wasn't giving up that easily. Wardi, the new housekeeper, was busy banging pots together behind the swinging kitchen door.

"That you, Miss Emily? You upstairs so long, I didn't know you home."

"Mmm, yes." Emily studied a small stack of mail on the dining-room table while Julian pushed into her side with his nose. Her lessons were thankfully over for the day; her tutor, Miss DeBoer, was gone shopping with Emily's mother.

"Your father says he's working late." Wardi backed through the door with a china soup bowl in her arms. "So we eat when your Mrs. Parkinson gets back in an hour or two."

"All right, then," Emily decided when Julian nudged her once more. "I'll have just enough time to air the dog."

"I don't think that's good idea." Their housekeeper frowned. "A young girl, out alone?"

"Oh, come now, Wardi. I won't be alone. I'll have Julian to guard me." Emily smiled up at the dark Egyptian woman as she clipped the end of her dog's leash to his studded leather collar—easier said than done, of course, as the 150-pound Great Dane danced in circles. He knew what was coming next.

"If anything happens to you—"

"If anything happens, I'll have Julian scare them away." She winked at their housekeeper. "Just don't tell anyone he hasn't any teeth left."

Emily skipped out the front door, nearly swept off her feet by the eager pull of the giant dog. There could be nothing better than a long walk with Julian.

"I'll be back!" she called over her shoulder, slamming the big front door shut with her loose foot.

"Dinner at half-past five, Miss Emily!" Wardi said something else, but Emily had taken off like a kite behind Julian. That gave them at least two hours, maybe more. With his giant tongue already flopped out to the side of his mouth, Julian was hot on the trail of a new scent.

First they plowed down Ben Maimon Street, past shops that used to be filled to overflowing with fresh-baked pastries, bouquets of bright flowers, even magazines and sweets from London. Now the shelves were as bare and lonely as Jerusalem streets after dark. Someone had scrawled *Brits Go Home* in dark, crude letters over the top of the *Spinney & Sons, Ltd.* sign at the shop where her mother used to buy Australian butter.

"Troublemakers," she whispered without thinking. That's what Father would have said.

They stayed clear of the guard stations set up at the corner of Gaza Road and Ben Maimon Street, and again at the big intersection where Ramban Street and Mamillah Road met the wide King George Avenue. Emily and Julian knew how to get around the guards. They ducked into an alley behind the Terra Santa College and popped back out on King George, which would lead them straight down to Plummer Square, and beyond that, the Yemin Moshe neighborhood, where her aunt Rachel lived.

"Slow down a little, Julian." Emily tried to hold back, but the dog was a downhill freight train. "I have a side ache."

Julian looked up at her with his big eyes and sloppy tongue, as if to say he was having the time of his life—which he probably was. A lorry rumbled by filled with British soldiers who stared at Emily. She turned aside to look at a faded flower skirt in Yossi Meir's Fine Dress Shop and Alterations window. Only a few more blocks to Aunt Rachel's house. She could already make out the old Montefiore windmill and the red tile roofs of the neighborhood at the end of the road.

Beyond that, of course, lay the Old City walls, and for a moment, she let herself wonder about Dov Zalinski.

It's his own fault, and none of my own. The thought didn't change the fact that no one had been able to tell her anything about his family. But what did she expect? It had been only a few weeks. This kind of search took months, she knew.

She also knew the chances of finding Dov's parents were slim. Or worse.

He could have stayed in Europe, she told herself. *He probably would have been better off there. Maybe he could have even gone to England.*

But no. Dov wasn't going to England. *She* was, and soon. He would stay; she would leave.

"Oh, Julian," she sighed as they reached Aunt Rachel's cheery front door. "It's just not fair."

Julian knew nothing about fair. His big hind end waved with his tail as he waited for his friend to open the thick-paneled door of Number 3 Malki Street. Emily noticed the climbing roses around the arch still had quite a few bright pink blooms. Aunt Rachel could sweet-talk a bloom out of a briar patch, no matter what time of year it was.

"Well, well, come in, come in!" Aunt Rachel's clear face lit up in a smile the moment she opened the door. "How's my favorite niece, and my favorite Great Dane, besides?"

Julian woofed his happy greeting and would have launched into Aunt Rachel's arms if Emily hadn't leaned back with all her weight.

Aunt Rachel just laughed. "All right, pal, I'll see what I can find for you."

That would mean a bite of leftover fat from a roast beef dinner, or perhaps a cracker. Once in a while, even a bone she had saved.

"It's your lucky day, my friend," said Aunt Rachel as she produced a large beef bone from a small paper sack under her kitchen sink. "Anthony has been trying to throw that thing away for almost a week. I keep telling him it's for a buddy of mine."

Emily loved the American way her aunt said things, the New York accent so unlike her own.

"He's in dog heaven." Emily grinned at the sight of Julian hunkered down on the cool terra-cotta blue-and-white tiles of the kitchen, attacking his prize. Then she remembered what she had come to talk about.

"Sit down, Em. Some tea? Or maybe you'll stay for dinner? Your uncle Anthony is coming home in a few minutes, and there's plenty of borscht."

Emily balanced on the edge of her aunt's flowered couch and shook her head. Not that she didn't like her aunt's beet soup, especially hot.

"Are you sure?" Rachel paused in the kitchen doorway. "I can telephone your mother to make sure it's all right. We haven't seen you very much lately. Not since we don't meet for Hebrew lessons anymore."

Emily smiled shyly.

"Yes, I know," her aunt went on, "when the student gets better than the teacher, it's time to quit."

"Aunt Rachel—"

"Ah-ah." A warning finger went up. "How many times do I have to tell you?"

"I'm sorry . . . Rachel." Calling an adult by her first name was hard to get used to. But then again, her aunt was far younger than aunts were supposed to be. Twenty-two? Twenty-three?

"That's better." When Aunt Rachel smiled, her dark, pretty eyes danced, and she flicked back a strand of her straight black hair. "But something is bothering you, isn't it? It's a long walk from Rehavia. You didn't just come to see if Julian had a bone."

By that time Emily's lower lip was quivering, and Rachel lowered herself to the couch beside her niece.

Don't cry, Emily ordered herself. Not now. She would have to talk fast before it all spilled out in a waterfall of tears.

"Oh, Aunt Rachel, Father said . . ." And she shoveled into the details. About leaving to go back to England. About the girls' school her parents wanted her to attend there. About her tutor, Mrs. DeBoer, leaving soon. Even about leaving Julian behind. Who else would understand? Not that Aunt Rachel could do anything about it. But at least it felt better just telling someone.

"Emily." Rachel scooted closer and put her arm around Emily's shoulder. "I'm surprised you've been able to stay here in the city as long as you have."

"I know all that." Emily rested her head against her aunt's shoulder. "But this is my *home*. You know I love Jerusalem."

"I know. So do I." Aunt Rachel stared out the window. "But you also know how *dangerous* things have become lately. Even to walk your dog, for goodness' sake. After what you went through with the kidnapping, your parents just want to protect you, don't you see? They want what's best for you."

A long pause.

"You know that, don't you, Emily?"

"I know."

"And what about your friends? Don't you miss them since they left?"

"Of course I do." Emily swallowed hard. "But I won't find them if we go back to Parkinson Manor. They're all from London or Edinburgh. I might as well stay here. You and Uncle Anthony are going to stay, aren't you?"

Aunt Rachel took a deep breath and looked straight at Emily with a troubled expression in her eyes.

"Your uncle and I are called to this place, Emily. This is our home. God's given us work to do in Jerusalem."

"So why not me?" Emily blurted out what she had been thinking ever since her father told her they would be going back to England. "What if I . . . what if I just stayed here with you?"

"Oh dear." Aunt Rachel sighed and shook her head slowly. "Emily . . . I'm afraid you don't understand."

"Yes, I do. I *do* understand." Emily saw her idea slip out of her fingers and shatter into a million pieces on the floor. Maybe it was a poor idea, but . . . "I wouldn't be any trouble to you. I could help—"

"I'm sure you'll be able to come back and visit us,

after . . ." Rachel searched for the words. "After things settle back down."

Meaning, *no*. Aunt Rachel closed her eyes for a moment, the way Emily's mother did when she had a headache. She glanced out the front window, reeled her arm back, and got to her feet.

Was that supposed to be her final answer?

"Oh, there's your uncle." Aunt Rachel glanced at her petite gold wristwatch and back out through the window. "A few minutes early."

Emily followed her aunt's gaze out to the narrow lane in front of the small whitewashed rowhouse just in time to see the top of her uncle's head bob by the window. If she hadn't paid attention, she might have mistaken him for her father— only Uncle Anthony was younger and a few inches shorter. His hair was lighter, as well, and most people didn't notice the worry wrinkles running across his forehead until he got up close.

"Rachel?" He pushed open the door with a grin. "Oh! Well, well. Lovely! Look who's here."

"Hi, Uncle Anthony." Emily rose politely and tried to dab the tears away.

"Was I interrupting something?" He burrowed his eyebrows at Aunt Rachel in what must have been a private signal.

"Of course not." Rachel shook her head and brightened when he pulled out a modest bouquet of yellow roses, the stems wrapped in green wax paper and tied with a red ribbon.

"For my wife . . . and my favorite niece!"

"They're lovely. Thank you." Rachel kissed her husband as she took the flowers. "I'll put them in some water."

"You're staying for dinner, I assume?" Always the host, Uncle Anthony echoed his wife's offer. A moment later he was on the phone to his brother, and of course that's when the trouble began.

That's where it always began.

"Listen, if you think we'd put her in any danger..." Uncle Anthony's voice raised a notch and heated several degrees.

Aunt Rachel motioned for Emily to join her in the kitchen as Uncle Anthony began to pace, pulling the large black telephone off its table in the hallway.

"Are you still there? No, no problem. I was just trying to tell you that we'll make sure she's all right. You worry too much. In fact, two of *your* men have been pacing the road in front of my home ever since I returned. Did you know that?"

Emily stood up to see what her uncle was talking about. Two of her father's men? She peeked out the little front window to see a couple of bored-looking young soldiers in the distance, around the corner and leaning against a low stone wall on the other side of the lane. She hadn't noticed anyone there before when she and Julian had first arrived.

"Routine? Well, fine, but I see them here all the time. I'd simply like to know *whom* they think they're protecting."

Uncle Anthony frowned into the receiver and ignored Rachel's desperate back-and-forth, palm-down hand signals to change the subject.

"No, I'm just the sergeant—oh sorry, *ex*-sergeant—who's doing what he can. . . . Fine, I don't have time for this, either. Get back to your meeting, then. Yes, send a car if you like. Seven o'clock. Fine."

He replaced the receiver harder than he needed to—didn't *slam* it exactly—just loudly enough for everyone to know he was displeased.

"I'm sorry," began Emily. She looked around to see if

Julian had finished his bone. She could hear a ferocious grinding from behind the couch. "I shouldn't have come. I didn't mean to—"

"Nonsense." Uncle Anthony put on a smile. "You're welcome here anytime."

"So is your father," added Aunt Rachel.

Emily knew they meant it, but still she shivered, remembering how stiff and awkward the two brothers had been the last time her father had come to visit.

INTO THE TRAP

Dov wondered what he would say when he arrived at Number 3 Malki Street.

"Hello, my name is Dov, and I was just wondering if you've seen my parents?"

No, he'd have to think of something else. He stumbled at the bottom of a dry gully in the Hinnom Valley, picked himself up, and began climbing. At a distance behind him, the Old City walls stood like a guard over every dusty step. Up ahead, a lone blue-green acacia tree spread its low but welcome umbrella of shade over a corner of road that ambled up to the heights on the other side.

Nobody told me I'd have to do so much climbing to get around this city.

The view on the upside was worth it, though; fifteen minutes later Dov glanced back over his shoulder to see the grand corral of ancient Old City walls. Big Jaffa Gate opened around to the north, to his left, while Zion Gate hid just out of sight to the east. Facing the smaller gate and outside the walls, a commanding church tower reached for the ever blue sky. *Dorm-something, wasn't it?*

Dov caught his breath as he stood in the welcoming cool of an olive grove on the lower chin of this small city within a city. The whisper of a late-afternoon breeze had picked up from the south, rippling up the valley and cooling his face.

This has to be the place, he told himself. He did his best to remember the directions the gabbai had passed to him in the alley.

"*. . . to a gateway with a Star of David in the arch . . . on the hill above. In the place called Yemin Moshe, under the windmill.*"

Finding the windmill part was easy. In the distance behind him and to the right, over a few red tile roofs, he could easily make out its shape. What was this, Holland? He saw the stone archway, too, with the carved Star of David at its top.

This was Yemin Moshe, all right. For the first time in days, he let slip a smile. Finally something was going right.

He wasn't as sure he remembered the address, though, and he made his way slowly along stone-paved lanes and wide steps lined on both sides by shoulder-to-shoulder two-story homes crafted of clean Jerusalem stone. Number 3 Malki should be close by.

He practiced his line quietly to himself, lowering his voice a notch. "The gabbai at the Hurva Synagogue told me you might help."

Would that be enough? Would he need a magic password? "They said you would—"

Dov stopped in midsentence, only a dozen steps from a solid wood door with a cheery green *3* above the door. He actually smelled the danger before he saw it; a wisp of cigarette smoke wandered his way from between two rows of buildings.

And at first he wasn't sure if the two British soldiers had seen him. But he pressed his back against the stone column of a fence post and held his breath. He hid, unable to move.

A minute went by . . . two. And still Dov listened.

But then he wondered. What did it matter, really, if they saw him?

"This duty is about as thrilling as watching paint dry," one of the soldiers finally commented in a scratchy voice, probably hardened by too many cigarettes.

He and his friend were still puffing; Dov nearly choked at the bitter smell when he peeked around the corner. If he'd wanted to, he could have spit on their backs from where he crouched.

"Yeah," replied the other. "This is the last time we let the sergeant talk us into guarding one of these Haganah houses."

Haganah? Dov's ears pricked up at the word.

"There 'e is again." The first soldier elbowed the other. "Peekin' out the window at us. As if we're just going to pick up and leave."

Dov looked, too, and sure enough, a white lace curtain fluttered in the window of Number 3 Malki Street. Obviously, the people inside knew someone was standing watch over their house. And obviously, the guards weren't going anywhere.

"Least 'e could do would be to invite us in for tea," said the second soldier, and they both laughed. "I'm gettin' thirsty standin' out 'ere all day."

Dov pulled back around to the far side of the stone column and wondered what to do next. Walk on by as if nothing had happened? Maybe. The soldiers didn't know him. Of course, he couldn't knock on the door now—at least not while the soldiers were standing there.

Or could he? Maybe if he could make his way down Malki Street without being seen, he could circle around the back. The way he *should* have come in the first place. What had the gabbai told him?

Over the stone fence, through the garden in back. Away from the front door.

Right. This could still work. Dov took a deep breath and stepped quietly away from his hiding place. He hugged the wall for the rest of the block, until he reached another corner. Left turn and then left again, and he stood peering over the top of a row of stone fences and postage-stamp gardens. The fifth one down would be the one, and he tried to think of an innocent-looking way to climb someone's back fence and sneak into their backyard. It wasn't even quite dark yet, and he knew it would be safer if he waited.

But he couldn't wait. He'd come too far to wait. So he bit his lip and crept along the outside edge of the fence, staying low. A back door in one of the small houses squeaked open, next door to Number 3. He ducked when he heard a splash of water and a clucking voice. Dov peeked over the top to see a melon-shaped woman in a faded floral-print bathrobe flinging a pail of water into the overgrown bushes outside her back door.

One backyard later, he stood behind the fence at Number 3 Malki Street. Like the others, this fence wasn't high—no higher than his shoulders. So with a quick glance around, he hoisted himself up, teetered on the brink for a minute, and tumbled over to the protection of the garden.

Only he hadn't noticed the iron hook.

"Oh! What. . . ?"

Instead of dropping quietly to the ground, Dov found himself dangling upside down from the top of the wall, like meat on a hook. It took a moment before he figured out what had happened: His belt loop must have slipped neatly over the top of a blunt iron hook. Part of an old gate hinge, maybe? He couldn't tell. All he knew was that the blood was running to his head, and the garden in front of him looked very odd from where he hung.

And then there was the dog next door.

"Shh!" Dov tried to quiet the howling animal as he wriggled to free himself. The dog barked more, like a foxhound on the hunt.

"Mitzi!" chirped the woman next door. "Mitzi! You leave that cat alone."

Dov desperately tried to free himself before the woman in the flowered robe found out he wasn't a cat. He swung his legs back over the wall but managed to hold on with only one heel. At least a small bush hid him from the back door of Number 3.

But the bush wasn't foolproof.

"Who are you?" a woman asked him in Hebrew. "And what are you doing here?"

"I, uh . . ." This was not how Dov had wanted to meet the people of Number 3 Malki Street. Even from his upside-down perch, he could see that she was young and dark haired and wore pretty blue shoes. He tried to clear his head, tried to say something, but he was getting very dizzy.

"Rachel," called the neighbor lady, Mitzi's owner. The dog still filled the air with her excited barking. "Are you—"

"Not to worry, Mrs. Levy. We're just fine over here."

Hardly. Dov did his best to wriggle free.

"Rachel?" Someone else called this time, from the back door of Number 3, only Dov couldn't quite see. This time it was a man, and he didn't sound very happy. "Is there someone out here, Rachel?"

"It's just a boy, Anthony." Her voice was soft.

There. Dov finally reached his left leg over the top of the wall, enough to anchor himself better, and . . . pull up.

What he saw made him wish he hadn't.

"You, there!" The British soldier coming around the corner pointed his finger in Dov's direction. Dov didn't wait to find out what the man wanted. He knew. And there was only one thing to do.

With a mighty jerk and a rip of his pants, Dov tumbled to the garden below. He glanced up just in time to see half a pant leg waving like a flag from the top of the wall as an arm reached over.

"Now, just a minute!" cried the woman in the garden.

"Stop right there!" the soldier cried as Dov scrambled to his feet.

"What's going on out here?" asked the man from the house as he stepped outside.

No question about it—there was no way to go back over the wall now, even if Dov had wanted to. Mitzi was in a frenzy next door, and a soldier was on the other side of the wall. Dov had only one choice. He put his head down and sprinted toward the back door of the little house.

"Excuse me," he grunted as he nearly bowled into the thin man standing by the door. More shouts behind him. If he could get out through the front door quickly enough, if he didn't run into anyone else . . .

"Stop, I say!" The man of the house was obviously English, not Jewish at all.

Dov held on to the side of his pants to keep what was left

of them up, though most his left leg showed bare. Five steps to the door, and—

A girl screamed from the small sitting room, and Dov again thought of his pants. He never should have come here. But there wasn't time to apologize—especially not when he heard a growl and a deep, powerful bark.

Not another dog!

He yanked the front door open and flew out onto Malki Street.

The other British soldier didn't see him coming until it was too late. Dov managed to sidestep the man and run.

Back through the archway, out of Yemin Moshe. Through the olive grove, now shady in the late afternoon. Down the rocky hill, down into the gully, through the Hinnom Valley, and back up the hill to the Church of the Dormition. He remembered the name now, but it did him no good.

Run! He didn't look back. He would have to find another way to locate his parents.

Big mistake. He scolded himself. *I should have waited until dark.*

And he would have to sew his pants back together some-how. Maybe Mr. Bin-Jazzi would have another pair.

"Explain to me what just happened here." Uncle Anthony's eyes were still wide as he stared down the narrow street in the direction the intruder had run. He looked to his wife, who stood in front of Emily.

"I'm sorry for screaming," Emily mumbled softly. She did her best to hold Julian by the collar. "I was down the hall in the sitting room, so I didn't really see anything except a flash.

Perhaps the back of his feet. I was startled."

"No one told us this one was coming." Aunt Rachel lowered her voice to a whisper—the soldiers still prowled the area.

Emily knew that people often came to her aunt and uncle's home. People in trouble, looking for help, running from the British. Jewish people. Maybe the illegal kind her father was looking for.

This one, though—had he been so desperate he couldn't wait for the cover of darkness? He'd been lucky Julian wasn't so quick on his feet anymore.

They turned and walked back into the house, and Uncle Anthony carefully bolted the door.

"Perhaps he'll be back." Aunt Rachel held up a shred of fabric. "He might want the rest of his trousers."

An hour later, Emily tried not to meet Shlomo's piercing eyes in the rearview mirror. She sat still in the backseat of her father's car, her eyes closed, while Julian rested his chin on her knee and panted. She didn't mind the dog's breath so much.

"Are you all right, Miss Emily?" The driver's question finally broke the silence.

"Tolerably well."

She didn't mean to lie; it just came out that way. But she could still feel her heart beating hard, after the fright in Aunt Rachel's living room.

"Your parents are worried about you, I don't mind saying."

Emily frowned. "They're probably going to send me away to England."

"I'm thinking that's a good thing, after what just happened."

After what just happened? Emily opened her eyes. She hadn't told her father's driver anything about the wild scene at Aunt Rachel's house. Not yet. Then how. . . ?

"Whatever do you mean, Shlomo?" Emily had to know.

But he only shrugged and glanced up in the mirror as they turned the corner to Alfasi Street. "All I'm saying is this city's no place for a British major's daughter. And it's going to get worse before it gets better."

THE WATCHERS

Sweeping. Dov flipped the end of the old broom as hard as he could, sending a cloud of dust out into the street. *Always sweeping. Always polishing.*

Even with all his junk, Mr. Bin-Jazzi probably had the neatest shop in the Old City—especially now with Dov's help. His candlesticks gleamed, and his back-room treasures were free of dust. Dov leaned for a moment on his broomstick, glancing around just long enough to notice the dark stare of a man not ten paces away. Dov recognized the nose, the face, the kaffiyeh, the khaki shirt. Atallah.

What do you want? Dov would have asked it, if only he had known the Arab words. All he could do was return the stare, wait for the man to look away and continue down the street.

Dov sighed and returned to his work. This Watcher wasn't the only one. Ever since Dov had returned from the disaster three weeks ago in Yemin Moshe, they had been watching.

Mr. Bin-Jazzi always laughed and said no, they weren't, but Dov was sure of it. They were there every time Mr.

Bin-Jazzi rolled up the tired green metal front of the shop, every time Dov returned from a delivery. They sat around street-side tables at the little restaurant across the street, drinking cup after cup of dark, steaming Turkish coffee and playing endless games of *shesh-besh*. All the time watching. When Dov warned his friend, Mr. Bin-Jazzi only smiled and reminded him of something that was written, something about not hating his brothers.

Fine for him. Dov was sure the Watchers didn't read the same book, didn't play by the same rules.

Still they watched, like the British soldiers outside the house where the gabbai had told him to go. Of course, Dov hadn't told anyone what had happened there, not a word. Only that he'd caught his pants on a hook, which was true, and that he had not been able to find his parents, which was also true. He also didn't tell Mr. Bin-Jazzi how hard it had been to slip by the British guards on the way back to the shop. And now, of course, there was no going back to Number 3 Malki Street.

"You should not worry so, my young friend," Mr. Bin-Jazzi told him, and then he told Dov about God feeding the birds of the air and caring for him. That was all very well for birds, Dov thought later as he again prepared to close up the shop.

The Watcher on the corner paused to look over his shoulder when Dov sent an extra-big cloud of dust after him.

"Eat dust!" Dov told the man in Polish, softly enough so that no one could hear him. But Dov's smile melted when he turned around to face Mr. Bin-Jazzi's frown.

"A bird of the air will carry your voice, young man."

"Pardon me?" Birds again! Mr. Bin-Jazzi was always talking in riddles.

" 'Curse not the King, no not in thy thought.' " Another soft voice joined in, this one smooth and steady, even with a heavy accent. " 'For a bird of the air will carry your voice, or some winged creature tell the matter.' "

What now? Dov turned yet again to face a brown-eyed pilgrim in a matching brown wool frock—the kind that covered his head in a peaked hood and reached down to almost drag on the pavement. A faded gold cord wrapped his waist.

"Solomon wrote about cursing the king," the man said. "And it would apply nicely to non-kings, as well, wouldn't you think, Farouk?"

"Father Samuel. *Abuna!*" Mr. Bin-Jazzi hurried forward. "What brings you here?"

A priest, here in the Muslim Quarter! Dov was certain the Watchers would notice this unusual visitor.

Not that the man's face gave him away; with dark eyebrows, high cheekbones, and a trim black goatee, he looked as much an Arab as Mr. Bin-Jazzi himself. But his starched black-on-white collar peeked out from under the man's cloak as if loaded with a metal spring.

"You will hardly believe my story when I tell you, my friend." The visitor patted his worn leather satchel and nodded toward the inside of Mr. Bin-Jazzi's shop. "Perhaps inside?"

"Of course, of course." Mr. Bin-Jazzi scurried to find the best seat in the shop, the one with four strong legs and a blue cushion. "Dov will bring coffee. How much sugar will you have, Abuna?"

"Oh, none, thank you."

Even if you wanted sugar, we don't have any to give you, Dov thought.

The priest smiled as he sat. "I didn't know you had an

assistant." He did not let go of his satchel as Mr. Bin-Jazzi introduced them. Father Samuel smiled and nodded politely, but it was clear his mind was somewhere else.

"Farouk, I don't mean to inconvenience you. But since our families have always been close, I knew that I could trust you with . . ."

His voice trailed off as a man walked slowly by the open shop door.

"Dov, the door."

Dov wasn't sure which door Mr. Bin-Jazzi meant—the outside metal roll-down door, or the set of double doors that usually stayed open during the day. So he jumped up and tugged on the short rope that pulled down the big metal door. It stuck, or Dov wasn't heavy enough to pull it down. Either way, he hung a half foot off the ground, nose to nose with one of the Watchers.

"We're closed," Dov croaked in English. *"Masa al-khayr."* He used the Arabic words Mr. Bin-Jazzi had taught him for *good evening,* as if that would tell everyone it was dinnertime.

"Masa al-khayr," Dov repeated, but the shopper didn't act as if he understood. He stared past Dov at the priest, the man with the satchel.

"Here, let me help you," said Father Samuel. In a single tug he brought the roll-down door—and Dov—to the floor.

"Uh . . . thanks." Dov scrambled to his feet and hurried upstairs to fetch coffee for the two men. He could imagine the other man still outside, wondering.

He wondered himself when he returned with steaming china cups of thick Turkish coffee—almost thick enough to stand up a spoon, just the way Mr. Bin-Jazzi liked it. But the shopkeeper didn't even look up; he and his friend sat hunched over a small table studying a yellowed, book-sized piece of parchment, perhaps a skin, carefully laid out on a black velvet cloth. They whispered to each other in excited Arabic.

"What is it?" asked Dov, hovering behind the men.

Mr. Bin-Jazzi's hands shook as he leaned closer. He squinted through a pair of watchmaker's magnifying glasses.

"With a name like Dov"—the priest glanced up—"you would be able to read Hebrew, no?"

"Some."

Mr. Bin-Jazzi did not touch the small skin parchment, which had cracked and faded with age. Fragments had already torn away from the edges. But he pointed at a row of faded letters with the top end of a fountain pen.

"What does it say?" asked the priest.

Dov squinted, but he couldn't quite make out the lettering. It looked like Hebrew, all right, but different.

"It's . . . really faded," he told them.

"Faded, but not yet silent," said Mr. Bin-Jazzi. "Here. I'll get you started."

He started at the top right corner, moving right to left. Dov didn't even know the shopkeeper knew how to read Hebrew. But then again, Farouk Bin-Jazzi was full of surprises.

" 'And they shall bring all your brothers.' " The shopkeeper translated the words carefully, in a hush. " 'To my holy mountain Jerusalem. Out of all nations.' "

Dov looked up to see Mr. Bin-Jazzi wipe the tears from his eyes. Father Samuel squeezed the shopkeeper's shoulder as they continued to read, word by faded word.

" '. . . upon horses, and in chariots, and in litters, and upon mules . . . from one new moon to another, and from one sabbath to another, shall all people come to worship before me,' says the Lord."

Father Samuel pushed his black-rimmed glasses up to the

top of his forehead, and for a moment Dov thought he, too, would break down in tears.

"Do you know what this is, Dov?" asked the priest, catching a sniffle.

Dov leaned closer. The words sounded familiar, yes, and now he could make out a few of the letters.

"The book of Isaiah the prophet," whispered Mr. Bin-Jazzi.

"I knew that," said Dov. Even so, he couldn't see why the men were acting so strangely.

"I'm told it and others were found by a couple of Bedouin shepherds in a cave overlooking the Dead Sea," explained Father Samuel, replacing the glasses on his considerable nose. "Taken to an antiquities dealer in Bethlehem, who may not have recognized them for what they are—or could be. I acquired them . . . shall we say . . . at a modest price."

"So the rumors are true." Mr. Bin-Jazzi wrinkled his forehead.

"Perhaps true." Father Samuel wasn't convinced yet. "What have you heard?"

"Nothing much." Mr. Bin-Jazzi shrugged. "A few weeks ago a friend at the university called to ask if I knew anything. All he said was that he'd heard something old had been found."

"So these aren't like your fake scrolls," Dov blurted out.

Father Samuel covered a half grin. "That's why I'm here, as a matter of fact. They may be the most important scrolls ever found. Scrolls old enough to help prove the truth of the Bible as we read it today. Or . . ."

"Or . . . ?" Dov asked.

"Or they may also be very clever fakes. Forgeries. Like Farouk's tourist scrolls."

He picked up a couple of Mr. Bin-Jazzi's souvenirs and held them up.

"The one you brought looks real to me," admitted Dov. He had never seen anything so ancient looking.

"As it does to me." Father Samuel pushed his chair back from the table. "But I'm a priest, not an expert in antiquities, as you are, Farouk. I believe you can determine if these are as real as we hope they are. In any case, I will leave them with you for the time being so that you may examine them."

Mr. Bin-Jazzi's hands were still shaking. But he carefully folded the scroll back over with Father Samuel's empty pen, then replaced it reverently in the cloth pouch in which it had come before he lowered it into the leather satchel with the others. For good measure he kissed his hand and touched the outside of the satchel softly.

"Promise me one thing." The priest's expression grew deadly serious. "You will not mention to anyone what you have in your hands. No one else knows of this, not even back at Saint Mark's. It is too dangerous."

"Abuna!" Mr. Bin-Jazzi looked up with wide eyes. "You know I would never—"

"Say no more." Father Samuel raised his hands and smiled. "I am sorry. I should not have mentioned it. But the boy . . . remember how a bird of the air carries the voice?"

"I trust him completely." Mr. Bin-Jazzi grew just as solemn. "He is no thief. And there are no birds in this shop, eh, Dov?"

Considering what the shopkeeper had called him just over a month ago, Dov thought the words sounded odd, though they made him feel good. Father Samuel left his treasure on the table for them, pulled his hood back over his head, and stood. "I shall pray for you, my friend." He looked serious, but once again his eyes sparkled as he yanked up the metal door with a quick movement and slipped out.

You'll need to, thought Dov. *You don't know about the Watchers.*

The priest turned to look at Dov as if he had heard the thought. "And you, as well, my new friend. There is more in these scrolls than perhaps you know."

What is that supposed to mean? Dov nodded and noticed one of the Watchers across the street, leaning against the corner of Hadawi's restaurant and slowly running a string of yellow beads through his hands.

The priest hurried down the street and disappeared into the gathering evening shadows along Ha Shal-shelet. Most everyone else had pulled down their roll-down doors for the evening, and Dov could smell the delicious aroma of frying falafels.

"What is that you kept calling him?" Dov asked as they lowered their door. "Abu. . . ?"

"Abuna." Mr. Bin-Jazzi smiled as he gathered up the satchel. "It is what you call a father or a priest whom you love and respect. Abuna. Father."

Dov repeated the word quietly and wondered. The two cups of Turkish coffee he had prepared for the men sat untouched.

THE WATCHERS
RETURN

12

"Q, R, S, T . . ." Emily sighed, licked her fingertip, and pulled apart the paper form before slipping it into its proper place in the file drawer. Not that she minded helping at her father's office in the afternoons, after her lessons with Miss DeBoer were over. She'd been doing it for years. And he always told her how much of a help she was.

It's just that in the three weeks since she'd been to her aunt's house . . . well, she'd hardly been able to walk Julian without her father worrying.

"Emily, are you all right?"

"Are you still there, Emily?"

"Just checking on you, dear."

The major peeked out his door every few minutes, just to make sure, she supposed. She even thought she'd heard him answer a telephone call from her mother, who was checking on Emily, too.

"Yes, dear," he said in his telephone voice. "Emily's still here. I just checked on her. She's fine."

Emily had to pause and smile. Dear Father. She had just

returned to her filing when the door behind her—the door to the outside office—burst open.

"Miss Parkinson!" Lieutenant Phipps gasped and came to a halt next to Emily's filing cabinet. As he caught his breath, he quickly straightened his trim-fit uniform and ran a hand over his hair. He seemed to know exactly how good he looked. "Is your father in?"

Emily checked the closed door to her father's office, but she didn't even need to knock as the door swung open.

"Emily, could you—" Her father stopped when he saw his aide. "Oh, Phipps, where have you been? I have several cases to review with you. Step inside. I'll check on you later, Emily."

"Right away, sir." The light-haired lieutenant seemed happy to hurry inside. Maybe he had planned it that way. "And I wonder if I might also share with you something I've just learned. Quite important, actually. It's about . . ."

The door clicked behind them, but it did not shut out the hum of the two men's voices, growing louder and louder. Emily found a stack of letters near the door that needed straightening.

"I'm well aware of how important a discovery it may be," said her father a few moments later. The irritation in his voice was obvious, even through the door. "But I'm afraid this is neither the time nor the place."

"Begging your pardon, sir," replied Lieutenant Phipps.

Emily had to lean closer to make out what he was saying.

"But I believe this is the chance of a lifetime, and all perfectly legal, naturally, or I would never bring it up. In fact, my contact says—"

"Your *contact*? You make this sound like a spy adventure."

"Oh, but it's my job to know, sir. In fact, I have a very

good informant inside a Muslim terrorist gang. I'm fairly certain they're collecting weapons."

"That doesn't surprise me in the least."

"Of course not, sir. But the Arabs want to get their hands on these scrolls only to sell them. For a fortune, I might add, which would mean they could buy even more weapons. In any case, they do *not* want the Jews to possess these scrolls. So if we can get to them first—"

"There you go again!" thundered the major. "You assume this scroll nonsense is all true."

"I wasn't sure before. Now I'm nearly certain there's something to the rumor. They're called the Qumran scrolls. Qumran is by the Dead Sea."

"I know where Qumran is. But I will have no more of this . . . Dead Sea Scroll foolishness, or whatever you call it."

"Begging your pardon, sir, but it's not foolishness. I'm told the scrolls are in the hands of a Syrian Orthodox priest named Father Samuel. He's at Saint Mark's Monastery in the Old City. With your authority, sir, I could probably claim the scrolls for the Crown. And the whole 'adventure,' as you call it, would be over."

"That's all fine, Phipps. However, we have enough business of our own to finish up without getting muddled in amateur archaeological ventures."

"But, sir, if we play our cards right, we might even share a bit of the credit. Imagine walking into the Explorer's Club back in London, sir. After everyone forgets the rumors, we're Major Alan Parkinson and Lieutenant Neville Phipps, discoverers of the Dead Sea Scrolls."

"Lieutenant!"

"All right, then. If you're not interested in the fame, sir, then certainly the money involved might be most attractive. I'm certain we could sell—"

"That is quite enough. Now, I do not want to hear another word about these scrolls. And from now on, you will concern yourself with other matters. Do I make myself clear, Lieutenant?"

Major Parkinson's words seemed to echo before Lieutenant Phipps squeaked his answer.

"Perfectly clear, sir, and naturally I meant no impertinence. I merely thought—"

"You will leave the thinking to me, if you please," snapped the major. "Now, take those requisition files with you on the way out. That is all."

"Sir."

A red-faced Lieutenant Phipps stepped out a moment later, mumbling to himself.

Emily held her breath as he hurried by.

"You had your chance . . . *sir*," he whispered. "Now it's up to *me*."

Emily stood statue-still behind a large metal file cabinet. The lieutenant did not notice her there, but the clerk from the front office did.

"Oh, there you are, Emily." The clerk held a large binder. "I was just looking for you."

"Me?" Emily mouthed the word quietly, pointed to a stack of papers, and did her best to look busy. "I was just straightening up here."

The lieutenant glanced back in surprise. He wore the look of a scolded puppy, rather than his usual sunny grin. Could he tell Emily had been listening at the door?

"Well, dear, we may have found your missing person." The clerk tapped an entry in her binder with a pencil and glanced shyly at the lieutenant. "This just came in from Cyprus, so I thought I'd come up here to tell you myself."

Wasn't this the same clerk who had shooed her away the first time Emily had asked about Dov's family? But when the clerk batted her eyelashes at Lieutenant Phipps, Emily understood.

And when the lieutenant turned around to join them, the clerk didn't seem to mind.

"See here?" She smiled at Lieutenant Phipps as she flipped a page for them to see. "Normally this would have taken months. But this letter says that a . . . Mordecai Zalinski from Warsaw was registered in the Cyprus detention camp. That *was* the name you were after, wasn't it?"

Emily nodded. *So Dov's father is all right?*

"Excellent work, Miss . . ." Lieutenant Phipps wrinkled his forehead while the woman's cheeks turned sunset red.

"Sleigh." She finished his sentence with a sickly sweet smile aimed at the floor. "Olive Sleigh."

But her smile froze as she checked the columns again. "Oh," she whispered. "That's strange."

"Something wrong?" Emily tried to read the chart, but her eyes lost the way down a column of tiny numbers.

"Oh dear," the clerk gasped. "I'm afraid that explains why we received this information so quickly. I hadn't realized."

Emily didn't know what Olive Sleigh was talking about. Even Lieutenant Phipps ran his finger down the page, and he frowned.

"He's quite well, then?" Emily was afraid to guess the answer to her question.

Olive Sleigh didn't say anything, so the lieutenant picked up the chart himself.

"It appears this person, ah . . . passed away there in the

camp," he said. "In any case, he never made it to Israel."

Passed away? The news hit Emily like a slap, even though she had never met Mordecai Zalinski before, never even seen his picture. She closed her eyes and remembered the way Dov had talked about his family, about his father. Little-boy memories, but very real.

"Are you certain?" Emily asked. People made mistakes, after all. With so many refugees, who could tell?

"Quite certain, dear. See right here?" Olive pointed her painted red nail at the name, and this time she actually looked pained. Or perhaps *embarrassed* was the better word, considering the lieutenant watching her. "I'm sorry."

Dov knew the Watchers would come back, no matter what Mr. Bin-Jazzi said. So when two of them strutted toward the shop a few days later, he already knew what he would have to do. Even before they had walked into the store, Dov had slipped behind the curtain.

"Mr. Bin-Jazzi!" Dov hissed. "They're here again. Those men!"

The shopkeeper jerked his head away from the scrolls and looked at Dov with weird, magnified eyes. He glanced quickly toward the front of the store, flipped off the magnifying lenses, and patted Dov on the shoulder.

"Whatever are you hissing about?"

"The men, the ones who wanted to hide their guns here. Atallah and his friends. They're back!"

They had to be in the store by now. Dov could barely whisper the words. And how did he know they wouldn't just follow him back here behind the curtain? They hadn't shown the best manners the last time they'd visited.

"Don't worry, boy. I'll talk to them again. Will not be a problem."

"But—" This time Dov was thinking about the treasure, the scrolls. Mr. Bin-Jazzi had spent enough time with them by now to know they were quite real, and if the scrolls were real, then they were surely valuable. And if they were valuable, then perhaps the men had heard about them. Secrets were hard to keep in the Old City.

Someone coughed in the front of the store.

"Just a moment," Mr. Bin-Jazzi called out. "I'll be right there."

Mr. Bin-Jazzi had said more than once he wasn't worried about the scrolls—not the way Father Samuel had been. But he paused before pushing aside the curtain to the front shop and gazed back at the parchments on the table.

"Perhaps you should put them away somewhere," he whispered. "Wrap them in the velvet cover and put them in the satchel with some fakes. See that you're very careful."

Dov did as he was told while Mr. Bin-Jazzi greeted the men in front. Right away, he knew this time was as bad as their first visit, and now Dov understood a few words.

"Silah." That meant *weapon.* And Mr. Bin-Jazzi said "no" a lot. So they were still arguing about hiding the guns. Dov didn't dare peek; he just stood in the middle of the back room with the leather satchel in his hand, wondering what to do.

Should he hide it upstairs in their little apartment? No, they would be sure to look there, if they looked anywhere. And he would be trapped, besides. But then, they would be sure to search the back room, too.

He could think of only one place, and the idea made him shiver.

The cisterns!

He knew there wasn't much time; the argument in front was growing louder. He could only guess what they were saying.

Quickly Dov moved to the back of the room, where Mr. Bin-Jazzi had stacked four or five heavy wooden crates. He put down the satchel to push, and he grunted as they slowly moved aside.

Quiet! The slightest noise would give him away. One more foot, and Dov had the boxes arranged in a half circle around the front of a wooden trapdoor in the floor. They would not be able to see him now from the front.

He could not see a thing anymore; the lone bulb hanging from the ceiling by the curtain shed only a weak circle of light that ended at the crates. Dov groped along the floor on his hands and knees, wishing the men in front would just go away.

He knew they wouldn't, and though he wasn't sure what they would do if they found the scrolls, he was sure he didn't want to find out the hard way. He scrambled along the stone floor until his fingernails caught an edge. . . .

There! The trapdoor! How many years did Mr. Bin-Jazzi say it had been since it had been opened? No matter. He dug down hard and came up with splinters.

A second time. The voices were growing louder. Finally the old door edged up, only a crack, but enough. He planted his fingers like a knife blade and pried, and then he was hit by a musty draft of air.

Open. The door was open!

But one problem remained. Wouldn't the men see the door and follow? Obviously. So he pulled up the lightest of the surrounding crates and tipped it up on the edge of the now half-open trapdoor. It would settle down on top of the door after he slipped through. The trick would be to climb down with the satchel without getting squeezed in the process.

"Silah!"

A voice coming through the curtain nearly pushed him through. With one hand he held the narrow door open, with the other he gripped the satchel.

I just hope there's something to stand on down here.

He swallowed the lump in his throat and pointed his toes. He would need a ladder of some sort to rest on, just like . . .

And then it hit him that he had done nearly the exact same thing before, only in another place—back at the kibbutz. He had tried to forget about hiding in the well when the British soldiers had been looking for illegal immigrants like him.

Only this time no one was after *him.*

I just hope Mr. Bin-Jazzi appreciates this, he thought.

Dov heard the curtain snap aside just as his foot found some kind of rope ladder to rest upon. He let the door lower slowly over the top of his head.

Safe for now, he told himself. In a few minutes the men would leave, and he would simply climb back out to safety. Mr. Bin-Jazzi would give the scrolls back to his friend the priest, and things would be back to normal.

He heard muffled footsteps above his head and guessed whoever had entered the back room was poking among the crates. Looking for the scrolls, or perhaps a place to hide his guns? The footsteps faded and Dov began to relax—until his rope ladder twitched.

The old rope gave him almost no warning. With a sudden jerk, it snapped, and a moment later Dov was falling backward into the blackness.

LOST IN
THE CISTERNS

13

Dov awoke to darkness and felt pain in the back of his head.

Am I dead? He honestly wasn't sure. His arms and his legs moved, but he couldn't see his hand in front of his face. And the throbbing pain would not let go.

"Ohh," he groaned when he felt the bump. That at least told him he might still be alive. If he was, though, not a sliver of light squeezed through the trapdoor above. He had no way of knowing how far down he lay.

He felt around on the damp stone floor of the cistern. His tailbone hurt, too, but everything seemed to work. His hand brushed against the satchel with the scrolls.

Good. Although when he thought about it, it was the satchel that had got him into this mess.

Or was it the rope? He needed something or someone besides himself to blame for being stupid enough to climb down into the cistern. How long had it been? A day? An hour? Ten minutes?

The tangled rope remains next to him gave no clue. But

it might tell him how far down he lay.

A foot . . . he measured off the ancient ladder, hardly more than string in places.

And I trusted my weight to this thing!

Two feet, three . . . he guessed as he passed it through his fingers, hand to hand.

Nine . . . That was all of it. Enough of a fall to crack his head. He was sore, yes, but he could stand, and he waved one hand above in the blackness.

"Mr. Bin-Jazzi?" he whispered. He heard nothing back, only a faint scrambling sound off in the distance.

What about the rats Mr. Bin-Jazzi had warned him about?

No, he told himself. *There can't be any rats down here.*

But still he wondered. And as he listened for rat sounds, he lined his back up to one of the walls, trying not to think of what he might run into or step on. He began counting again, this time heel to toe.

"Eleven, twelve . . ."

The echo of his own words almost made him jump. Even his breathing echoed. Would they hear him up above? What if the visitors to the shop were still there?

"I don't care."

When his toe hit a rock, he bent down to collect it. He held it in his hand and looked up, trying to find a clue to where the door opened in the ceiling.

Nothing.

"Hey!" he yelled.

"Hey . . . hey . . . hey," echoed the walls. He waited for the sound to die down.

"Down here!"

"Here . . . here . . . here," replied the walls.

"Mr. Bin-Jazzi! Are you all right?"

"Right . . . right . . . right . . ."

His forehead felt clammy, and he gripped his rock even harder to keep from shaking. This would not do. Before he could change his mind, he wound up and threw the rock as hard as he could, praying he might somehow hit the underside of the trapdoor. He ducked under a shower of sharp rock confetti as the rock he'd thrown bounced back at his feet.

"This isn't going to work," he mumbled, gathering the rock for another try.

"Mr. Bin-Jazzi!" he screamed.

"Jazzi . . . Jazzi . . . Jazzi," muttered the walls.

How could I have been fool enough to fall down here?

"Are you all right?"

More echoes.

"Mr. Bin-Jazzi!" he screamed at the top of his lungs. What was going *on* up there?

Nothing. Only echoes.

When Dov stomped his foot and gritted his teeth, he could almost see angry red streaks in the darkness. He leaned back and threw the rock as hard as he could, not straight up this time, but right at the enemy—the wall in front of him. He raised his hand to his face, expecting it to bounce back or maybe shatter into a thousand pebbles.

Nothing happened. He stopped to listen to a faint clatter—*bounce, bounce, bounce.*

A way out?

Dov gathered his satchel and followed the throw carefully, one hand in front, each toe slowly looking for a step. For all he knew, the floor might drop out from under him. How big had Mr. Bin-Jazzi said these things were? Big enough for an elephant bath?

But the tunnel—if that's what it was—seemed to lead

straight out of the cistern. This time he could touch the damp ceiling just above his head. And actually, the tunnel wasn't quite straight, and it wasn't clear, either. He ran into boulders every few feet, stony rubble that slowed and choked his way out. Even so, he was going somewhere, perhaps up a bit.

"I've got to find a way out so I can get back to see what happened to Mr. Bin-Jazzi," he told himself.

Twenty minutes later he followed a new discovery—light. Not enough to see where he was going, but enough to show a faint outline of his hand, and then enough to show him when he had finally come out of the tunnel. Was this another cistern? If it was, this one was half filled with crumbled old Roman columns and boulders. The mess left him just enough room to climb a narrow stone stairway built into the side wall.

"Almost there." He paused to see where the light was coming from, and for a moment he panicked. What if he couldn't get out of this one, either? At the top of the stairway, he faced another trapdoor, much like the one he had come through from Mr. Bin-Jazzi's back room. The difference this time was that dim light streamed from around the edges.

And this one appeared to be nailed shut.

"Oh no." Dov sank down to his knees, inches from the edge, and tried to keep from sobbing. So close, but . . .

He could pound on the door until his knuckles were raw, but who would hear him? So he slid back down the stairs to find himself the largest rock he could carry.

If no one hears me, I'll hammer my way out.

No matter that his arms ached with each swing. It felt good to connect with a part of the world of light. And he kept hitting until the wood began to splinter, breaking apart more and more. A crack, and he finally heard the squeal of a nail pushing through wood planks.

One more time! He swung until two boards loosened and the door in someone's floor gave way.

A minute later he had crawled through the hole and lay panting on the floor of a small, dim room. But even dim was much brighter than he had endured over the past while. He covered his face and had no idea where he was—until he heard footsteps coming closer.

"Did you hear that?" asked a young voice on the other side of a door.

Dov lay on the floor and smiled. Not so much at the sound of the voice but the language.

Hebrew.

And that could mean only one thing.

He had burrowed his way from Mr. Bin-Jazzi's shop on Ha Shal-shelet to the Jewish Quarter!

"Who are you? What are you doing here?"

Dov heard but at first could not see. He squinted and shaded his eyes at the person in the doorway. Only after his eyes had gotten used to the light could he make out the long, curly locks of an Orthodox Jewish boy.

"Look, Reuven." Two others crowded into the room and pointed at the broken floorboards. They looked a lot like the first boy, each with a pair of glasses balanced on their noses. These two held books in their arms, as well.

At last Dov could see they were a few years younger than he was. Just kids! He guessed he had perhaps stumbled into a *yeshiva*, a Jewish school for boys.

"Go get Rabbi Simeon," said the first one, holding the other two back with his arm. They all wanted a look at Dov.

"That would be just fine." Dov stood up with the satchel in hand. "I need some help, you see. I think Mr. Bin-Jazzi may be hurt, and—"

"He's an Arab!" cried the smallest of the bunch, and they backed away from Dov as if he were a leper. Two of them turned around to run. The leader stumbled backward and tried to slam the door.

"No, wait!" Dov lunged after them. "Let me explain."

The three boys were almost too quick, but Dov managed to wedge the toe of his right foot into the door just before it slammed.

"Ow!" Dov wrestled with the doorknob. "Listen, I'm Jewish. I work in Farouk Bin-Jazzi's shop, but I'm Jewish, just like you. And I need to get out of here."

"Rabbi Simeon!" screamed the boys.

Do I look like an Arab? Dov wondered about the clothes Mr. Bin-Jazzi had given him. Maybe he did.

Finally Dov pushed hard enough and tumbled out into a classroom. A solid wood table crowned with piles of hefty leather-bound books was ringed by well-worn benches, some of them matching. On the far side of the room, a door framed by two dirt-fogged but sunny windows looked as if it might open to the outside street—and freedom.

But Rabbi Simeon's young students mobbed around, peppering him with questions. Dov wasn't sure where the rabbi himself was; maybe it was lunchtime.

"Why are you here?"

"Who sent you?"

"Are you an Arab spy?"

Dov shook his head and pushed toward the outside door. Almost there . . .

Everyone froze at the sound of a solid ruler slapping a table. Hard. That explained all the jagged pockmarks on the tabletop.

"WHAT is the meaning of this OUTBURST?"

Rabbi Simeon, if that's who it was, had no trouble securing the attention of his young students.

Dov didn't dare look back; he took the chance to slip toward the door.

"Pardon me," Dov mumbled to no one in particular. "I must be going."

And with a move he had practiced many times before in the past few years, he scooted sideways and around the two boys who remained between himself and freedom. A second later he was sprinting down the crowded street.

Any direction would do just now. But the boys' shouts followed him.

"Catch the Arab spy!" they yelled as they spilled out the front door of the yeshiva. "Don't let him get away!"

Sorry, boys. Dov looked back to see students pouring out into the street, too late, of course, to catch up with him, but not too late to catch the attention of two young British guards on patrol in the neighborhood.

"You there!" cried one of the guards.

The way he held his rifle left Dov no choice. He froze while everyone on the street stared at him or backed away into the shadows. They had obviously practiced this sort of drill before.

"Why the rush, young chap?" The guard sneered over the butt of his rifle. "Perhaps you need some help?"

I need some help, sure. Dov did his best to look casual. He dug his free hand into his pocket and held the satchel behind his back with the other. *Only not this kind of help.*

But the scrap of paper he felt in his pocket gave him a desperate idea.

THE LIEUTENANT'S MISSION

14

"Phipps here."

Emily tried her best not to stare from across the office as she finished her filing, but the lieutenant's voice had a way of carrying across the room, especially when he was on the telephone.

"No, the major is out for the day," Phipps continued. "I'm his aide. But his daughter . . . I see."

Of course Emily's ears pricked up at the word "daughter."

"He has *what?*" Phipps looked across the room and signaled for Emily to join him. "Yes, that's curious. How in the world. . . ?"

Emily put down her folders.

"And *Emily Parkinson's* name?" He laughed. "You're certain? Perhaps I can clarify that immediately. She's right here, in fact. Hold the line, Sergeant."

Lieutenant Phipps cupped the telephone in his hand and looked at Emily as if to tell another of his jokes.

"Miss Parkinson, a couple of our boys over in the Old City just picked up a young lad with a rather odd scrap of paper in his pocket. With your name and address."

Emily's mouth turned dry. *Dov Zalinski!*

"What's even more queer is that the boy says he knows you, which I should doubt, of course." Phipps studied her expression. "Nevertheless, we shall have to treat this as a rather serious breach of security. Perhaps you could shed some light on the matter?"

"Um . . ." Emily cleared her throat. "That is, I . . ."

Lieutenant Phipps watched her for a moment with his eyebrows arched, then returned to his phone conversation. "Heavens no, she hasn't the foggiest. But of course we'll take care of the matter for you."

He was about to hang up but caught himself. "Pardon me—say that again? What kind of old parchments?"

The amused smile on the lieutenant's face disappeared, and his voice faded to a whisper.

"Are you sure? Describe them. Yes, it's important. What are they wrapped in?"

He listened, his eyes growing wider and wider.

"That's not possible. Those parchments are—oh, never mind."

He listened for another moment.

"All right, then, listen to me. I'll be there in fifteen minutes, but hold on to the parchments until we get there. Do you understand? The boy? I don't care. What?"

He frowned and chewed on his lower lip.

"All right, fine. If it makes you feel better, tell him we'll send someone to check on this Bin-Jazzi fellow later. But the parchments are the important thing. Under no circumstances is *anyone* to touch *anything* until I get there. Do you understand me? Good."

He slammed the receiver down, looked around the near-empty office, and picked up the phone once more. A moment later he was speaking to someone else in a low voice.

"Listen to me carefully," he whispered. "Where has the priest been in the past twenty-four hours? Has he been out with the . . . ah, items?"

Lieutenant Phipps tapped the toe of his shoe as he listened.

"All right, so you're saying there's a chance he could have taken them somewhere? Right. And what's the name of that shopkeeper friend of his? Ben . . . Yes, that's it. Did you tell me he has a boy? Ah, this is starting to become very interesting."

He motioned for Emily to come closer.

"Now, listen carefully, my friend. This may be nothing, or it may all have just fallen into our laps. In any case, I want you to meet me at this Bin-Jazzi's shop on . . . right . . . in exactly one hour."

Lieutenant Phipps hung up the phone and grabbed Emily's arm in almost the same motion.

"I'd like you to come with me, young lady," he said as he whisked her down the stairs to the main office. "You may be able to help us identify this lad, clear up a few things."

"But—" Emily started to object. Phipps wasn't listening. "Olive," he called over his shoulder. "If anyone else calls, I'll be at . . ." He looked around the office, then shook his head. "Never mind, Olive. Good-bye."

"Could you tell me what's happening?" Emily tried to keep up with the lieutenant as they jumped into his car.

By that time his grin had returned. "You have no idea, do you?"

Emily shook her head.

"The less you know, the less trouble it will be for you."

Emily had an idea her father would not approve of Mr. Phipps's mission, after what she'd heard. She squeezed her eyes shut as the lieutenant pressed the gas pedal to the floor and they shot through a second busy intersection.

"There's just one thing I still don't understand," he began, ignoring the honking of a truck he had just flown by.

Emily's fingers clamped the handle in front of her. She peeked at her white knuckles.

"The boy—" he passed a checkpoint at the wide Jaffa Gate to the Old City with a wave at the guards, "exceedingly odd that he should have your address—but I'm sure we'll straighten things out."

Emily was afraid they might. And she had her own questions—and worries.

What will I say to Dov? she wondered. *He won't believe me when I tell him about his father.*

They screeched to a halt in front of the Kishle Police Station, not far inside Jaffa Gate and across the street from Christ Church. For a moment Emily's mind wandered to the time she and her parents had attended a wedding there—a woman from her father's office. But that was before things had become more . . . difficult . . . in the city.

She doubted the lieutenant was thinking about church. He jumped out, leaving his car door open; he didn't even check to see if Emily was following.

"I suppose you'd like me to come in?" Emily shrugged and followed, curious.

The street entrance to Kishle looked more like a large tunnel than a door—a covered driveway guarded on two sides. One of the guards recognized her and smiled.

"What are you doing here, Miss Emily?" he asked.

"The lieutenant was on some business." She pointed in

the direction of the station door. Was Dov still in there? She wasn't sure she wanted to know. All the same, she mounted the steps and paused at the front door. "Er, was a young Jewish fellow brought in a little while ago?"

The guard nodded.

"Kicking and screaming, 'e was."

"Did you hear him say anything?"

"Only something about an Arab chap who needed help." The guard shrugged. "They let him go just before you got 'ere."

"WHAT IS THIS?" Lieutenant Phipps had no trouble making himself heard, even through the front door of the station.

Dov or no Dov, now Emily was sure she didn't want to go inside. She paused with her hand on the brass door handle.

"Glad I'm out here and not in there." The guard winked.

Emily cracked open the door and peeked inside.

"I thought I made it perfectly clear to Jenkins." Lieutenant Phipps waved a handful of yellowed pieces of paper in the air. "And where is he *now*, pray tell?"

Emily didn't quite hear the answer, only the lieutenant's explosion.

"Off DUTY? I told him I was coming right over. And he has the nerve?"

Emily heard a few more withered words from the new officer on duty.

"Wonderful." The lieutenant didn't mean it, of course. "Sergeant Jenkins told you to mind the parchments, did he? And this is what you give me?"

"I didn't know..." The small man at the desk tried to explain.

"You didn't know? Do these look like the most valuable

parchments in history to you?" The lieutenant waved the yellow paper in the man's face. "These are fakes, corporal. FAKES! The kind they'll sell you in the Old City market for a few shillings. And you let the boy leave with the real ones!"

"But Jenkins said you didn't care about the boy. We had no grounds to hold him."

Lieutenant Phipps moaned, held his forehead with one hand, and crumpled the papers in the other.

"I want to know how so much *damage* could have been done in such a short time. No, don't answer that. Let's just locate the boy again. Do you hear me?"

Emily backed up and let the door swing quietly shut. Someone called from behind her.

"Emily!"

Emily knew who it was without looking.

"Emily, over here!"

She turned to see Dov standing between two army trucks in the small entry courtyard. He gripped a satchel in one hand and waved at her with the other. Her friend the guard hadn't noticed yet.

"Emily?" boomed the lieutenant from the other side of the door. Had he finally noticed she wasn't with him? "Where's the major's daughter?"

She hopped down off the step to meet Dov before the station door could open. Dov looked her in the eye. "I never thought I'd be glad to see you again," admitted Dov. "But I could use your help to get out of here."

He glanced at the guard at the entry to the courtyard. "Please, I have to get back to the Street of the Chain," Dov nearly begged her. "I'll explain everything later."

Emily looked at him for only a second; Lieutenant Phipps

would come out to look for her in a moment. "Come on, then."

With a shy smile she quickly led the way past the guard.

"It's fine, I know him."

The guard looked carefully at the odd couple, then back at the station door.

"Would you please inform Lieutenant Phipps not to wait for me?" Emily guided Dov by the arm. "I'll find my own way home."

The guard nodded. "Do be careful, then, Miss Emily."

She waved cheerfully and skipped out through the entrance ahead of another outbound truck. She would have some explaining to do later but thought it was wise to act naturally for now.

"Hurry," she whispered, but Dov didn't need the advice. They skittered across the street in front of the station, side-stepping a honking car.

"Emily!" She could barely hear Lieutenant Phipps over the sound of a delivery truck lumbering behind them. "Emily Parkinson!"

They ducked into the courtyard behind Christ Church and around the corner of a guesthouse, out of sight.

"Come on," she told Dov. "There's a way through here."

"This way." Emily pulled Dov to the side at the sight of another pair of soldiers.

He was glad to follow, though he was amazed that she knew her way around so well. This maze, this Old City . . . even after nearly two months here, he found himself easily turned around. He had never delivered supplies for Mr. Bin-

Jazzi in this neighborhood, that was sure.

Mr. Bin-Jazzi! Dov quickened his step to keep up. Already he had taken too long to return to the shop. He was afraid to think of what he might find when they arrived.

They hurried down one alley and up another, through a rusty iron gate that screamed on its hinges, under a low archway choked with flaming pink climbing roses. Where were they now? Maybe still in the Armenian Quarter, where they began. Or perhaps they had crossed over into the Jewish Quarter.

"I suppose you don't know where we are?" Emily asked, a half step ahead.

That was the Emily Parkinson he remembered. Stuck up, bossy, and obnoxiously English. Why was she helping him? To prove how much better she was?

"You think I don't know where we are? Of course I know. We're in, ah—" Dov looked up to see a cross in the window—"the Christian Quarter."

Dov would have expected Mr. Bin-Jazzi to live in this neighborhood. But then, Mr. Bin-Jazzi didn't do what people expected him to do. Maybe that was his problem.

"Hmm." She didn't slow down. "I suppose that was an easy question."

"How do you—"

Emily laughed and finished his question. "How do I know my way around? I grew up in this city, remember?" They turned down another shadowy alley, lined on both sides with tall stone walls and only a few narrow windows set high above. "My friends and I used to play chase through here. But you still haven't explained to me why you need to get to Ha Shalshelet."

Dov had to tell someone. So he told her about the men

who wanted to store their weapons in the shop and how they had found out about the scrolls. . . .

"So you really do have some valuable parchments? I heard what Lieutenant Phipps said, but—"

"I didn't leave all the parchments for your lieutenant." He patted his satchel with a grin. "They belong to someone else."

"He's certainly not *my* lieutenant. But you're more clever than I thought."

He supposed that was the first compliment he had heard from her. As they hurried from alley to alley, he explained how he had found the cistern and how Mr. Bin-Jazzi hadn't answered his shouts.

"Bin-Jazzi?"

"He's the man we're going back to help," explained Dov. "I work for him in his store. He's going to help me find my parents."

"Bin-Jazzi . . ." Emily quickly gave him a strange look. "Lieutenant Phipps mentioned that name. We'd better hurry."

Emily explained what she knew of Lieutenant Phipps, how he had disobeyed her father's orders, and what he was doing to try to steal the parchments.

"I'm afraid to ask," Emily looked over her shoulder down a narrow cobblestone lane, "but how did Mr. Bin-Jazzi get these scrolls? And if they're so valuable, why are they in an old leather satchel?"

"A long story." That would have to be enough for now. He raced through the Old City streets as fast as his legs would move.

"This is it," Dov finally told her. The sight of the rolled-down outside metal door told Dov that something was wrong at the Golden Rock Factory for Olive Wood. Mr. Bin-Jazzi rarely closed that door during the day.

"Mr. Bin-Jazzi?" Dov's hand shook as he rolled up the unlocked front. "Are you in there?"

"Dov, wait." Emily touched his arm. "Don't you think we need help? What if—"

"No help." Dov shook her off and pushed open the inner door.

"But no one's here," pronounced Emily. "That's a good sign, isn't it?"

"Not really." Dov shook his head. "He could be upstairs."

Dov swallowed hard and drew back the curtain to the back room.

"Mr. Bin-Jazzi?" he croaked. His heart jumped when he saw the slumped figure in the corner.

STREET RESCUE

15

"Oh dear," cried Emily as she and Dov both knelt next to the still body of Mr. Bin-Jazzi. "Is he. . . ?"

Dov fought off the horrible feeling in the pit of his stomach and leaned a little closer. He had to know.

Even the shadows couldn't disguise the man's injuries. Poor Mr. Bin-Jazzi had been hit in the face, hard, and more than once. And Dov knew exactly who had done such an evil thing. He picked up the man's hand, and his own tears fell.

But the hand was still warm!

"I think he's alive." Dov rubbed the man's hand gently. He thought he heard a low groan. "But I don't know how long before . . ."

He couldn't finish the sentence, afraid that even thinking the thought would look like an invitation to any angel of death waiting just outside the shop door. If he could have stood between Farouk Bin-Jazzi and this angel, he would have.

"Not yet!" Dov raised his voice and rubbed the man's ragdoll limp hand. "He's not ready!"

"What are you going to do?" Emily asked.

"We have to get him to a hospital."

Emily nodded and stood. "I'll go—"

"No." It was Dov's turn to take charge. "See that delivery cart over there? You take his legs."

"You're not serious. We're going to cart him away in *that*?"

"You have a better idea?" Dov began to scoop Mr. Bin-Jazzi gently up by the shoulders.

"You don't think someone in the neighborhood could help us? Doesn't he have friends?"

"They're all scared," Dov grunted as together they lifted the man carefully into the cart. A wool tapestry would cushion his ride, and the satchel could serve as a pillow.

"Scared of what?"

"The men who did this. Trust me. It's up to us to help him."

Emily nodded and helped to push the delivery cart toward the storefront.

"Now, open the doors and let's—"

A British lieutenant stood in the doorway.

"You, boy, are standing in my way." The smile on the lieutenant's face looked forced as he rested his hand on the leather holster of his revolver. Behind the lieutenant, a tall man in a khaki shirt planted himself on the street, his arms crossed. There was no mistaking his face.

Atallah! What was a British officer doing with—?

"Emily," continued the lieutenant, "I don't know what you're doing here, but your father is not going to be pleased at all. In fact, I'd wager he'll be quite angry."

"Not as angry as when he hears the truth about you."

"Oh dear." He shook his head but kept the smile on his face. "How little you understand."

"I understand enough to know you're not following orders." Emily squeezed her hands into fists, as if she would pummel the lieutenant. "Now, you let us go."

Atallah chuckled in the background.

"Of course we'll help your friend," Lieutenant Phipps crooned as he edged forward. "But first I need to see those parchments."

Three feet from your greedy hands, thought Dov, and he braced his foot for what he knew might be Mr. Bin-Jazzi's last hope. Surely this lieutenant would not help Bin-Jazzi, and neither would Atallah. Not when it was Atallah who beat him up!

"So, will you give us the scrolls now, or . . ." The lieutenant softened his voice and held out his hand. "Or would you rather have my friend, er, persuade you?"

"I'm going to tell my father!" Emily stomped her foot.

"I'm sorry, dear, but you're going to have to think of a better idea than that." The lieutenant's plastic smile never left his face. "You father isn't going to tell me what to do anymore. Oh, he'll miss me at first, but he'll get over it. Now that I've found what I'm looking for, I don't need him, you see."

"You're a deserter!" she gasped.

"Ah, but if only your father had just . . . joined in, things could have been quite different. We could have been rich and famous, I expect. Now I'll be glad to settle for simply being rich, but I do require your assistance, young lady."

Emily's eyes narrowed and she clenched her fists. Assistance?

"Phipps!" Atallah didn't seem to like the way this conversation was headed. "The parchments!"

"My dear Atallah." Phipps turned back for a moment. "You don't seem to understand the finer art of—"

Dov took his chance. With a grunt he pushed the cart with all his strength—straight at the door and Lieutenant Phipps.

At first Emily thought Dov had gone berserk. But it took only a moment to realize this was her chance to escape, too. Would Lieutenant Phipps let her walk away after what he had just told her?

She thought not.

So she grabbed the side of the delivery wagon and pushed, too—hard. Lieutenant Phipps cried out in surprise as the cart caught him in the back and rolled over him like some sort of road-building machinery, but Atallah was a bit quicker. He managed to skip back a step and tried to slam the door in their faces. But by that time they were picking up speed, and the end of the cart slammed into the door, hurling it back at Atallah and launching him backward into the street.

"Don't stop!" Dov ordered, but Emily had no thought of even slowing down. Not while these two were anywhere close by.

"Don't worry," she answered as they peeled around to their left and hurried down the busy Street of the Chain. "We'll get your friend to the hospital."

The task would have been much easier if the streets had been wider, level, and free of people. At least going downhill was easier than trying to push the other way.

"Coming through!" Dov shouted as they barreled closer to a narrow spot in the lane shaded by canopies and crowded full of after-dinner shoppers. "Hather!"

Emily tried to drag her feet to slow them down. One of

her black shoes flipped off behind them.

"Dov, we can't—" Emily gripped the side of the cart, closed her eyes, and lifted her feet off the ground.

A woman in front of them screamed, setting off a chorus of excited shouts.

"I can't stop!" yelled Dov, and Emily waited for them to careen into the crowd ahead.

But like the Red Sea, the crowd of shoppers parted to either side as they railroaded through the Suq. Or at least, Emily assumed that's what had happened when they came out the other side. It was a second later that she dared to peek.

"How about that?" Dov grinned. "I think we made—"

The canopy that hit Dov in the face was the size of an umbrella, but the brass merchant must have strung up half his goods on the canopy, creating a beautiful display of brass lamps, bottles, and bowls. A dozen or more now dragged along behind the cart like anchors, even after Dov managed to untangle the canopy from his face.

The brass merchant himself gave chase, shouting and waving his fist at them.

"Faster!" Dov did his best to push them past a small set of stairs set into the side of the street.

Emily put her hand down to keep Mr. Bin-Jazzi's head from hitting the side of the cart. She looked back.

"Don't look behind you now."

Dov did anyway. They both saw Atallah's determined face as he pushed past the brass merchant.

"Right!" Emily commanded, and they almost didn't make the turn into a narrow alley. Atallah was getting closer.

"And left!" Another near-miss. She thought she remembered the way to the French-run Saint Louis Hospital, just outside the New Gate by Allenby Square. Just outside the Old City walls.

"I'm sorry I got you into this," Dov muttered as they screeched through another turn on two wheels.

"It's not your fault." Every breath scorched her lungs as she gasped for breath. Had she heard the tough Jewish boy right, or did her ears play tricks on her? *He* was sorry? Dov was never sorry for anything.

By that time, Atallah was only ten, maybe fifteen paces behind them. They had reached the top of another small hill and were about to roll down. Saint Louis Hospital was just around the corner and through the New Gate.

"Just a little more . . ." Dov's face was flushed, too, and he barely managed the words.

She wasn't sure what the man would do to them out here on the street. She honestly didn't want to find out. At that moment their brass anchors broke loose, tumbling behind them. Dov barely managed to hurtle over them.

"You take it!" Dov yelled as he handed over his grip on the cart's handle.

"What?" At first Emily didn't understand, though she managed to steer the cart down the hill.

"Go!" Dov waved her on and turned to face the man who chased them.

Emily had her hands full directing the cart to the Old City wall, toward the gate that would take her and Mr. Bin-Jazzi to safety—assuming he was still alive.

She took one last look over her shoulder as Atallah flew over the crest of the hill, then waved his hands desperately, kicking his feet in the air.

He must not have seen the brass lamps and bowls piled on the street.

ABUNA

16

"Dov? Dov Zalinski?"

Dov felt a gentle hand on his shoulder, and he rubbed the sleep from his eyes. For a moment he couldn't imagine where he was, not until he focused on the starched white dress of the nurse leaning down to wake him.

"I'm Dov." He stretched his aching muscles and tried to get up off the waiting-room floor. He couldn't remember falling asleep. . . .

"Shh." The nurse put a finger to her lips after she helped him to his feet. "You really shouldn't be sleeping there, but you look so tired."

"What time is it?"

"After midnight." She fished about in her striped apron pockets for something. "And I had almost forgotten. This is for you."

"Me?" He didn't know if he should take the envelope she held toward him. How did she know who he was?

"The young lady left it here for you before her father came to get her." The nurse's smile convinced him. "They had to leave. But she sounded quite sure you would show up."

Almost didn't. Dov didn't want to tell her what had happened last night in the Old City streets. Didn't want to tell anyone—especially not how close Atallah had come to cornering him in an alley, back in the maze on the other side of the Old City walls. The brassware had slowed Atallah down, but not for long. Dov was just glad he could climb better than the Arab man. For now he was safe—as long as Atallah decided not to follow them into the hospital.

"Thank you." Dov took the envelope as the nurse turned to go. He stuffed it in his back pocket.

"Wait a minute!" he blurted out. "What about Mr. Bin-Jazzi? Is he all right?"

"Mr. Bin-Jazzi is resting down the hall, room twelve." She looked at him and tilted her chin to the side. "You're not . . . related, are you?"

Dov paused only a moment before he straightened his shirt and limped in the direction of Mr. Bin-Jazzi's room.

"Not exactly." He lowered his voice. "But I work for him."

She looked at Dov curiously but didn't stop him. And as he headed down the hall, he decided he would keep watch over Mr. Bin-Jazzi for as long as it took for him to heal. Emily was gone, after all, and who could say if Atallah would come into the hospital, or Lieutenant Phipps? He slipped into room 12 and paused at the door to let his eyes adjust to the shadows. *Which one?*

Dov heard the raspy breathing before he could tell which of the four beds Mr. Bin-Jazzi slept in. By the weak glow of a night-light he finally made out a round bundle of bandages neatly framed by pale blue hospital sheets.

That would be Mr. Bin-Jazzi's head. Dov could see the

man's closed eyes, his bruised nose and lips, but the rest was mummy-wrapped. At least he was breathing! Dov had never known Mr. Bin-Jazzi's snores would sound so wonderful.

Or so weak.

He took up a station next to the bed and tried to find a comfortable way to slouch into the straight-backed vinyl hospital chair. And he waited, listening for each breath that signalled Mr. Bin-Jazzi still lived. After each one he wasn't sure he would hear another, so he tried to breathe at the same time—as if he could breathe *for* him.

Breathe.

They breathed that way for an hour or more, together, until Dov felt light-headed, dizzy. He lost track of time. After a while Mr. Bin-Jazzi snored again, then coughed weakly.

"You're going to be all right, sir," Dov whispered. "Please live."

He knotted his fingers and sat helplessly at the side of the bed, trying to think of words to pray, magic words he could say to make the man better. But his mind only knotted up as tightly as his fingers, and all he could feel was pure red-hot hate for the men who had done this to them.

Hate for the Nazis who had taken Dov's family and scattered them to the wind. Hate for the neighbors who had closed their windows and their ears to the cries of their Jewish neighbors—almost like the neighbors on Ha Shal-shelet, who closed their eyes to what Atallah and his murdering thieves did.

He couldn't forget the greedy English Lieutenant Phipps, either, coming into the Old City to steal the ancient scrolls that didn't belong to him.

"I hate them all. The Nazis, the English, the Arabs . . ."

Dov picked up a pair of scissors next to the bed and

gripped them until his hands hurt.

"Let them come back now," he whispered and gazed toward the sliver of light from the open door. A dark thought brushed his mind, one that made him shiver with cold, but he let it stay. "Let them try to get past me. They'll be sorry."

He waited for the sound of footsteps coming down the corridor, the click of shiny military boots. Instead, he heard the murmur of nurses checking their patients, a soft laugh now and again, the drone of a radio, someone reading the news in English. He jumped at the touch of a hand on his.

"Yaa!" He twisted in his chair to face Mr. Bin-Jazzi. The scissors clattered to the cold tile floor.

"Mr. Bin-Jazzi!" he whispered. "You're alive! I mean, I'll get a nurse."

Dov began to rise, but Mr. Bin-Jazzi raised his hand to hold him back. Dov remembered how the man's grip had once been so strong. Now . . .

"Reports of my death were exaggerated," croaked the man in the bed. His eyes fluttered open, and they glittered with tears in the half-light. Mr. Bin-Jazzi flashed a faint gold-toothed grin. "I am still alive. Stay here."

"Sir." Dov moved closer.

"They're about to vote!" announced one of the nurses out in the hallway.

Dov didn't care too much about what a scratchy-voiced Englishman said on the radio, but he heard more scuffling out in the hallway as people came to listen.

"Ooo, the United Nations vote," said one woman, hurrying to hear the broadcast. It sounded like a roll call.

"Australia," droned a hollow English radio voice, very, very far away.

"Yes," answered another radio voice.

"What's this foolishness?" Mr. Bin-Jazzi's voice faded into the shadows, into raspy breaths.

Dov decided the man must not be talking about the radio broadcast but about being in the hospital. "It's not your fault—"

"That's not what I mean." A cough. "I'm talking about *you*."

Me? thought Dov. *What is he talking about?*

"Bolivia," continued the radio voices.

"Yes."

"Canada."

"Yes."

"Egypt."

"No."

And Dov again: "You . . . you should rest, sir."

But Mr. Bin-Jazzi would have none of it. He stared at Dov in the darkness of the room, and he would not let go of Dov's hand.

"You, Dov. You sit here and shake your fist in the air."

"No, I—"

"Don't lie to me, boy. I heard it all this past hour. My eyes were closed, but my ears were open."

Dov swallowed hard. Here? Now? Had Mr. Bin-Jazzi really heard everything?

"Great Britain."

"Abstains."

On it went, country after country. Some no, others yes. The nurses' station outside was silent as they all listened to the radio. What was all the excitement?

And still Mr. Bin-Jazzi gripped Dov's hand.

"Tell me, Dov Zalinski . . ."

He closed his eyes, and Dov thought he had fallen asleep once more.

"United States?" asked the radio voice.

"Yes."

"USSR?"

"Yes."

At that, Dov heard a whoop and clapping out in the hall. He peeked out to see two nurses dancing arm in arm around their radio. The nurse who had given him the letter stood and bounced on her feet, looking as if something very grand had just happened.

Outside their window Dov heard the same thing: cheers, shouts, clapping, and then dancing. Why was everyone so excited?

But Mr. Bin-Jazzi was not finished yet. "You tell me, Dov Zalinski, how long have you lived in my shop, eating my bread?"

What?

"I . . . I'm not sure," Dov stuttered and looked out the door for the nurse. "A month? Two?"

"Eight weeks and six days."

"Oh." Another gulp.

"And in this time what have I told you about hating your brothers? What did Isa al-Masih say?"

Dov remembered the words— *"Whosoever hateth his brother is a murderer"*—but he could not, would not, repeat them aloud.

Not yet.

"You remember, Dov."

"I remember, but—"

"But nothing. You know the words. Don't be stubborn. He waits for you, Dov. Don't make Him wait too long, eh?"

The words turned to less than whispers now, fading fast. "And one more thing for me, Dov."

"Yes?" But Dov wasn't sure he could obey.

"Return the scrolls to Father Samuel for me, eh? You know what they are . . . and who else wants them."

"I know."

"Only be careful."

Dov sucked in his breath as the words sunk in.

Mr. Bin-Jazzi squeezed his hand. "Will you do this, my son?"

"I will. I promise."

"Just don't, please don't, make Him wait . . ."

Make who wait? Father Samuel? Bin-Jazzi's God? And wait for what?

But there were no answers. Mr. Bin-Jazzi's eyes had closed once again.

Dov glanced down at the dark floor where the satchel rested. He picked up the scissors by the handles and replaced them gingerly on the table. Strange. He hardly wanted to touch them now. The hot rage had drained away, and Dov could not get it back if he tried. Not here, next to a wounded, forgiving Farouk Bin-Jazzi.

Then it struck him—what had Mr. Bin-Jazzi called him? *"My son"*?

Maybe he'd heard wrong, but he hoped he hadn't. Not that this man could ever replace Dov's father. Oh no. But no one besides Imma and Abba had ever called him "son" before.

"Please don't die . . . Abuna," he whispered, and he meant it as a prayer for Mr. Bin-Jazzi.

Abuna . . . Father.

Actually, if he was honest, Dov knew the prayer was for him, as well. Because as he stood there in the dark hospital room, staring at Mr. Bin-Jazzi, he realized he desperately needed this broken, beaten Arab man. Maybe just a touch of the love and forgiveness that flowed so easily from him. Maybe he could be more like him.

But could I ever really be like him? Would I even want to?

No. At least, not yet. Why would he want to be so weak? Dov stroked the man's wispy hair to the side and placed a damp hand towel on his forehead.

Isa al-Masih . . . Jesus. That's who made Mr. Bin-Jazzi the way he was, Dov knew. It was no secret. Had Jesus given Mr. Bin-Jazzi love for the people who had beaten him to within inches of his life?

I could never be like that, Dov decided. It was strength that mattered. In his mind he replaced the picture of Atallah with the memory of those men who had torn his family apart. The big Arab man became a leering Nazi officer in a pressed black uniform and tall black boots.

"Men this way!" screamed the German officer as Dov had stumbled off a cattle car in front of the dark prison camp years ago. *"Women this way! Children over here! Hurry!"*

Hurry to live the nightmare. Hurry to work. Hurry to die.

No! It is too much to forgive, Dov thought. And it hurt too much to forget. How did Mr. Bin-Jazzi do it?

Dov wasn't sure. But as he watched Mr. Bin-Jazzi sleep, a strange idea crossed Dov's mind—that he should be the one lying there in a hospital bed, not his friend. He touched the man's hand, hoping perhaps he would wake once more, tell him what to do. For one unguarded moment, Dov knew he would change places with the man, if only he could.

He jumped when a nurse stepped into the doorway. A bright hall light seemed to set a halo on her red hair.

"They've finally done it," she announced in a high, giddy voice.

Done what? Dov looked up, Mr. Bin-Jazzi's last words still in his ears, echoing through the room.

"Just don't make Him wait too long."

"The United Nations voted for the Jewish state!" said the nurse. "Did you hear that? We're going to have a state!"

Without waiting for an answer, she fell back to her dancing in the hall with the others.

What did she say? Dov sat and watched as Farouk Bin-Jazzi returned to his shallow snoring. He wrung out the hand towel and replaced it on the man's clammy forehead. He could just see out the door into the hall now, to the end, where another door swung open. A tall, uniformed English officer stepped into the hallway.

Lieutenant Phipps?

Dov couldn't be sure, but he didn't want to poke his head out there to find out. He pulled the door to room 12 nearly shut before looking.

Turn around! Dov still couldn't see the man's face, hidden for a moment behind a nurse's peaked hat. Had the officer asked her a question? She listened, nodded, and pointed straight at Mr. Bin-Jazzi's room.

Straight at Dov! He ducked back. *How did he find me?*

A shiver ran up Dov's spine, but he knew what he had to do.

"I'll be back, Abuna," he whispered as he scooped up the satchel and hurried to the single window. Even over the chatter of the nurses, he heard the clicking of military heels coming closer.

NO ORDINARY NIGHT

17

"Come on, come on." Dov knew he had only one chance to swing the window open and get out of the room before Lieutenant Phipps, or whoever it was, came marching through the door.

The window wouldn't cooperate. Painted shut from the outside? He dropped the satchel to use both hands, and he felt the sweat on his forehead. For a moment he thought of sliding the satchel back under Mr. Bin-Jazzi's bed. So what if the English officer found it? It was really no concern of his.

But it was! Mr. Bin-Jazzi had asked Dov to return the parchments to their rightful owner, so that's what he would do. The window squeaked and groaned . . . but finally cracked open! He was out in a heartbeat and tumbled to the metal grate of the fire escape. He thought he heard a man's voice in the room behind him, but he couldn't be sure. Like a monkey swinging from one arm he slid down the stairs and dropped to the pavement below, still clutching the treasure.

"Dov!" boomed an unfamiliar voice high above his head. "Dov Zalinski. Stop there, boy!"

The voice only made Dov run faster, and he didn't dare look, didn't dare listen, didn't dare stop as he hurried through the darkness back toward the sleeping Old City. If he could get through it, Damascus Gate would take him into the Christian Quarter once again, to Saint Mark's Monastery, where he could at last free himself of the terrible old parchments, these Dead Sea Scrolls.

If only he hadn't promised!

"Dov Zalinski . . ." The voice faded behind him.

How did that man know his name?

Damascus Gate stood open but heavily guarded, so Dov kept walking south along the wall, just outside the Old City. On either side of the wall, Jerusalem at two in the morning was a very different place than the city Dov and Emily had flown through with their pushcart ambulance.

On an ordinary night, Dov knew the streets would have been turned over to packs of hungry-looking dogs, fighting and snarling over scraps left behind in the markets.

On an ordinary night, the shop awnings would have been rolled up tightly, the windows locked, dim lamplight traded for shadow.

And on an ordinary night, he would have been the only person on the street, except for the dozing soldiers.

But this was no ordinary night.

Dov pulled back at the first shout, wondering who else might be awake at this time.

Good, he sighed and kept to the cover of shadows. *They're not shouting at me.*

But the shouts came more often, and then he saw the circle of people, hand in hand, spinning in a *hora* dance, laughing and stumbling. More spilled out of a building, which now lit up as if for a holiday celebration. People, and more people, all with the same words on their lips.

"We're going to have a state! Our own state!"

They must have been listening to the radio broadcast, because just like the nurses in the Saint Louis Hospital, these Jews danced and hugged, cried and sang. One of the dancers grabbed Dov by the arm as he passed by on the sidewalk. Dov had no choice but to follow the circle around a time or two before he could break free.

"Dov! Stop!"

There—had someone called his name again? He wasn't quite sure with all the celebrating. Just to be sure, he darted behind a knot of people, doubled back around between two army trucks, sat on one of the olive green painted bumpers, and held up his feet. He could see Jaffa Gate just around the corner to the left.

He waited. No one came. The dancers got louder.

After a few minutes, he turned to a young man who twirled in a smaller circle with his girlfriend. Had the whole city emptied into the streets?

"Which is the fastest way to Saint Mark's?" Dov chanced the question.

"What?" The dancers both looked at Dov as if he had just dropped out of the sky.

"Saint Mark's. In the Old City." Dov repeated his question, but the young fellow shook his head.

"Are you crazy? You're not going in there." The young man frowned and turned away. "Didn't you just hear the news? The Arabs are going to be furious."

Dov stalked away from the hora dancers, wondering what

the news had to do with Saint Mark's, what it had to do with anything.

Fine. I'll find it myself. But first he had to get through Jaffa Gate, and guards stood at both sides of this entry, as well. He watched a few trucks pull up, check in with the guards, and rumble into the Old City. The guards' backs were turned; this would be his chance.

Now! He tucked the precious satchel under his arm and sprinted for the back of the next truck. Surely the back doors would be unlocked and he could slip inside.

They weren't.

He couldn't.

What now?

Dov would have scrambled out of the middle of the road, but a large gray car came up behind him just then, its head-lights projecting his outline on the side of the Old City wall. The car's back door flew open before Dov could escape to safety.

"Dov! Don't run away!"

Emily Parkinson's voice nailed his feet to the pavement as she hurried up to meet him. Dov held up his hand against the bright headlights, and she grabbed his wrist before he could change his mind.

"There you are!" It felt as if she wasn't going to let go of his arm without a fight. "We've been looking for you every-where. Why did you run from my father?"

"Your . . ." Dov looked at the man who stepped from the other side of the car. *The officer in the hospital?*

"No, please." Emily held on with both hands, and Dov could not pull himself free. "You don't understand, Dov . . . wait, no!"

Dov pulled away with all his strength, sending the satchel

flying to the pavement at the major's feet. Emily gasped. The man reached down, picked up the satchel, and held it out for Dov to take.

"Emily's told me about Lieutenant Phipps and the scrolls." The English officer frowned fiercely. "He had absolutely no right. And I promise you . . ."

His voice took on a steely tone.

"I promise you he will be found. And when he is, he will be disciplined severely. Deserters face serious consequences."

Dov took the satchel, and Emily moved back toward the car.

"Now, are you going to let us help you return the parchments?" she asked with a hint of a grin. "Or are you going to stay out here in the cold with all the crazy dancers?"

Dov hesitated for a moment longer, wondering if he would have been able to make it past the guards tonight. Major Parkinson held the door open. "I didn't come out here in the middle of the night for nothing, my dear fellow. Please get in."

Dov slipped into the long, dark military car, onto the velvet-textured seat next to Emily Parkinson and her father.

"I must tell you," the major continued, "Emily had to do a lot of talking to get me out here. I wasn't keen on the idea of going back to the hospital to look for you. But she *can* be persuasive when she sets her mind to it."

"Daddy!" complained Emily, and Dov could feel the warmth between the daughter and her father. He didn't mind sitting close to it, as if he could warm his hands by the embers of this fire.

"Right." Major Parkinson leaned forward to talk to the driver. "Let's take this young man to Saint Mark's, Shlomo."

The driver nodded and checked the rearview mirror as

they headed for the checkpoint.

"I'm so sorry about . . . your family, Dov." Emily started to pat the back of Dov's hand, once more clutching the satchel, but he pulled back.

He looked at her blankly. "What are you talking about?"

"Your family." She looked as puzzled now as he did. "The nurse at the hospital promised she would pass along the letter I received. Didn't she?"

"Oh, that." He reached back to pull out a wrinkled envelope with an official-looking return address. The British Ministry of Something or Other. He unfolded the paper inside. But what he read in the flickering light made him wish he had never met Emily Parkinson. A lump rose in his throat, and he strained to make out the words.

Dear Miss Parkinson, read the smudged, wrinkled paper. *In regards to your inquiry into the whereabouts of Mr. and Mrs. Mordecai Zalinski, formerly of Warsaw, Poland, we regret to inform you that Mr. Zalinski has been reported deceased at Detention Camp 3 on the island of Cyprus, where he was awaiting transport to Palestine. As to the whereabouts of Mrs. Zalinski, we can offer you no information at this time. Please feel free to inquire again in the future, should you require further details. Sincerely yours . . .*

He didn't read the rest. He didn't need to. Dov just crumpled the page, closed his eyes, and dropped his head.

His father, gone—if the letter was true, if he could trust it. Could he? And what about his mother? Surely Imma had not survived, if his father had not. But . . .

"It's not true," he whispered, mostly to keep himself from bawling. "It's not true."

But he knew it was. In his deepest heart he knew it was, and he had known it for weeks. Maybe ever since he had first visited the Hurva Synagogue and no one had heard of his family there.

And so his tears were overdue. Without knowing it, he had been keeping them for this time, a time he denied was coming. It made him think how Mr. Bin-Jazzi had cried telling Dov about the wife and son he had lost. For once, Dov didn't push away Emily's hand when it came to rest on his shoulder.

"I'm so sorry," she whispered. "But perhaps there's hope of finding your mother."

"Maybe." He wiped the tears with the back of his hand. "And my brother Natan, too, maybe."

Emily caught her breath.

"Did you say Natan?"

"My brother, Natan."

"Oh my." She held her cheeks in her palms as if she just remembered she had left the gas stove turned on at home. "I *knew* I should have saved that newspaper. But I think I have some good news for you. . . ."

EPILOGUE: ON THE MOUNT OF OLIVES

Emily waited silently at the edge of the Mount of Olives Jewish Cemetery, shivering under the gathering clouds of a darkening sky. She pulled the collar of her sweater up higher to hold back the cold breeze.

Most people had stayed indoors, it seemed, on this cold day in early December. And no wonder. She looked down the barren hillside filled with the memorial stones of generations, and across to the Old City and the towering Temple Mount and Dome of the Rock. Her mind wandered to what had happened near this spot, so long ago. To the time when all the people had cheered for Jesus, laying palm branches at His feet. Or the time He had spent here with His disciples, praying and singing, just before He died.

True, the view was a little different than when Jesus had walked this way, but she would have liked the chance to tell Dov a little more about what had happened on this piece of earth. Maybe she still would. He seemed more ready to listen now than before—surely more willing now than he had been with Henrik at the kibbutz.

Anyway, she *was* glad Mr. Bin-Jazzi was doing better. Glad, too, she'd been able to bring Dov the news that his brother Natan still lived, perhaps in Tel Aviv, on the coast. At least that's what the newspaper had said. She could have kicked herself for throwing away that copy of the *Palestine Gazette*, the one she'd picked up with the list of people who had changed their names. But she remembered it well enough. It was Natan *Israeli* they'd be looking for now, not Natan Zalinski.

A few steps away, Dov didn't seem to notice the cold. He kneeled on the damp earth to place a few memorial stones on top of the yellow letter. Without a grave on which to place the stones, it seemed the only right thing to do.

And as he spoke, Emily recognized parts of the *Kaddish*, the sad Jewish prayer of mourning. *"Yisgadal v'yiskadash sh'may raba . . ."* Which meant, *Glorified and sanctified be God's great name. . . . May He establish His kingdom in your lifetime and during your days.*

Dov prayed alone, not with the group of mourners tradition called for. But who would join him now? The bitter wind almost snatched the words from Dov's mouth. . . . *and within the life of the entire house of Israel, speedily and soon; and say, amen.*

Amen. Emily looked down the hill to the place where Shlomo had dropped them off, down by the beautiful Church of All Nations, next to the olive grove called the Garden of Gethsemane. And she added her own prayer that the words would soon come true in Dov's own life.

OF STREETS, TUNNELS, AND SCROLLS

Jerusalem in 1947 wasn't an easy place to live, but it certainly *was* exciting. History was being made nearly every day, as Emily and Dov found out in this story. Of course, sometimes it's harder to recognize history when you're living it!

What's real in this story? The tense conditions inside the city, to begin with. Jews and Muslims who had once lived together in peace began to compete more desperately for the same lands—especially when the British announced they were leaving Palestine soon. The summer and fall of '47 was especially tense.

All of the street names and places are real, as well. Places like the Street of the Chain and Malki Street in the Yemin Moshe neighborhood. The Hinnom Valley and the Church of the Dormition. The Search Bureau for Missing Persons is of course long gone, but it was actually there on King George Avenue. And the Hurva Synagogue today lies in ruins . . . but that's another story. Descriptions of that once-beautiful building are taken from eyewitness accounts.

The *Palestine Gazette* was real, too—even the names of the immigrants. So was the wording of the September 28 announcement when the British said they were leaving Israel. That's taken from an article in the *Palestine Post*. And the United Nations vote on November 29 happened very much as described.

Cisterns under the Old City also exist, something like they're described in the book. They're found underground in areas near the base of the ancient Temple Mount, in the neighborhood around Mr. Bin-Jazzi's shop. Even today, though, many layers of the Old City lie undiscovered. Perhaps there are other tunnels and cisterns, or maybe they're filled with stone and sand.

What about the Dead Sea Scrolls? They're real, too. They actually *were* discovered by Bedouin shepherds in caves overlooking the Dead Sea. You can visit the site of Qumran. And back in Jerusalem, the actual scrolls (parchments, really) have a permanent home in the beautiful Shrine of the Book Museum.

Besides that, Father Samuel of Saint Mark Monastery was a real person who helped care for the scrolls shortly after they were discovered. Our story's Father Samuel takes only his name from the real person and is not modeled on the man's actual personality, however.

The scrolls themselves turned out to be one of the most incredible archaeological finds of all time. Although there is still much to learn about them, we know they were copied by scribes belonging to a Jewish religious community called the Essenes sometime during the last half of the first century. Think about it for a moment—ancient scriptures were copied and hidden just as the Romans destroyed the Jewish temple, burned Jerusalem, and took the people away as slaves. The scrolls then lay silent for some 1,875 years, only to be discovered by shepherds . . . a year before Israel reemerged as a country. Talk about God's timing!

Exactly why the Essenes hid the scrolls in clay pots is still a mystery. But the scrolls contain portions of every Old Testament book except one (Ruth), and they're important because of their letter-for-letter accuracy to our own Bibles today—which shocked many people when they were discovered, especially doubtful scholars. Some had been saying that the Bible couldn't be trusted; they thought it had been changed by scribes over the years. Turns out the Scriptures hadn't changed a bit! And these scrolls prove God's Word has been kept true. They are silent no more . . . a treasure indeed.

FROM THE AUTHOR

Dov's and Emily's adventures don't stop with the last page of this book! Here are four ideas for you to try:

1. *Jump into the next adventure*, called *Brother Enemy*. Check out the preview following.

2. *Discover more books.* I've put together a list of some of my favorite books, magazines, Web sites, music, and more on Israel. They'll help you get a better feel for the strange and wonderful land Emily and Dov lived in. Be sure to show this section to your parents or teacher.

3. *Write to me.* I always enjoy hearing from readers, and I answer all my mail. (Or as Emily would say, my post.) How did you like the book? Did you have a question about anything that happened, or about what the characters were thinking? What's next? My address is: Bethany House Publishers, 11400 Hampshire Avenue South, Bloomington, MN, 55438 USA.

4. *Go online.* Visit my Web site at *www.coolreading.com*. That's where you can pick up writing tips from your favorite authors, share your ideas online, or even review a book. There's plenty of cool stuff to do at coolreading! Check out my bulletin board for the latest news, too.

That should keep you busy . . . until the next adventure.

Blessings!

Robert Elmer

WANT TO KNOW MORE?

You're in luck! The library, bookstores, and even the Internet are full of great resources for learning more about Israel and about the incredible events that happened there between 1946 and 1949. Here are a few ideas to get you started.

Picture Books on Israel

- *The Bible Lands Holyland Journey* by Dr. Randall D. Smith. Published by Doko in Israel, this is one of the better picture books of Israel and the Holy Land I've found. You'll see pictures of many of the places Dov and Emily visit.

History

- *The Dead Sea Scrolls* by Ilene Cooper (Morrow Junior Books) has details about the famous scrolls—how they were really discovered and translated, and who has claimed them over the years.
- *Israel: Enchantment of the World* by Martin Hintz and Stephen Hintz (Children's Press). A good overall introduction to Israel, this book has lots of photos and historical information.
- *The Birth of Israel* by Marlin Levin (Gefen Publishing House Ltd., Jerusalem). This unusual book is full of amazing color (!) photos taken during the 1940s. You'll see people celebrating their new state, marchers, street

scenes, and more—everything just as it was in Dov and Emily's day.

- *Zvi* by Elwood McQuaid. Zvi Kalisher's story inspired many of the events in Dov Zalinski's life. In fact, I had a chance to interview him personally in his Jerusalem home. The book is available through the Friends of Israel Gospel Ministry in New Jersey, P.O. Box 908, Bellmawr, NJ 08099. They also have an interesting magazine called *Israel, My Glory.*

- *The Creation of Israel* by Linda Jacobs Altman (Lucent Books World History Series, 1998). A good all-in-one history of how Israel was founded, this book has a useful time line, index, and pictures, too. A perfect resource for a student research paper.

Hebrew

- *Hebrew for Everyone*, published and distributed by Epistle. Here's a fun, kid-friendly approach to learning the language of the Old Testament—and today's Israel! The study guide is written by Hebrew believers in Jesus and is designed for kids and beginners. You can learn the Lord's Prayer in Hebrew! I picked up my copy at the Garden Tomb in Jerusalem for twenty shekels. (A shekel is about twenty-five cents.) Contact Epistle at P.O. Box 2817, Petach Tikva, 49127, Israel.

Internet

- *ChristianAnswers.net* is a good place to find out about the *real* tunnels beneath Jerusalem's Old City. Look for the answer to this question: "What is the truth regarding the controversial tunnel beneath the Muslim Temple Mount in Jerusalem?" at *www.ChristianAnswers.net/archaeology /home.html.*

- The International Christian Embassy of Jerusalem (*www.icej.org.il*) is a good place to connect to links to travel and historical information on Jerusalem and Israel.

Music

- *Jerusalem Arise!* (audio CD, Hosanna! Music). This inspirational CD has plenty of lively Hebrew-style worship songs. I often listen to this CD when I write! Recorded live in Jerusalem.

PREVIEW

Dov and Emily's thrilling story continues in book four of
PROMISE OF ZION, *Brother Enemy*.

It's 1948, Palestine is at a crossroads—and Dov Zalinski and Emily Parkinson are not sure which way to go. Dov continues to search for his family—or what's left of it. But the young Holocaust survivor has no idea what he would do or say if he somehow located his brother, Natan, lost during the war. Emily, on the other hand, has watched the city she loves turn ugly with violence. Still, how can she leave Jerusalem to go back to England, a place she barely remembers? As a new war draws nearer with each day, both Dov and Emily are in growing danger. Will their quests for family and home be in vain?

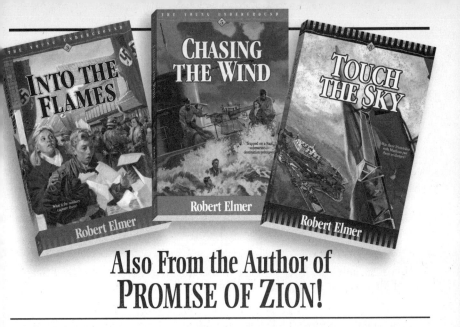

Also From the Author of
PROMISE OF ZION!

Boys and girls from all over the country write to Robert Elmer telling him how much they love THE YOUNG UNDERGROUND books—have you read them?

In THE YOUNG UNDERGROUND, eleven-year-old Peter Andersen and his twin sister, Elise, are living in the city of Helsingor, Denmark, during World War II. There are German soldiers everywhere—on the streets, in patrol boats in the harbor, and in fighter planes in the sky. Peter and Elise must help their Jewish friend Henrik and his parents escape to Sweden. But with Nazi boats patrolling the sea, they'll need a miracle to get their friends to safety!

Throughout the series Peter and Elise come face-to-face with guard dogs, arsonists, and spies. Together they rescue a downed British bomber pilot, search for treasure, become trapped on a Nazi submarine, and uncover a plot to assassinate the King of Denmark!

Read all eight exciting, danger-filled books in THE YOUNG UNDERGROUND!

A Way Through the Sea　　　*Chasing the Wind*
Beyond the River　　　*A Light in the Castle*
Into the Flames　　　*Follow the Star*
Far From the Storm　　　*Touch the Sky*

Available from your local Christian bookstores or from Bethany House Publishers.

The Leader in Christian Fiction!

BETHANY HOUSE PUBLISHERS

11400 Hampshire Ave. South
Minneapolis, MN 55438

www.bethanyhouse.com

Series for Middle Graders* From BHP

ADVENTURES DOWN UNDER · by Robert Elmer
When Patrick McWaid's father is unjustly sent to Australia as a prisoner in 1867, the rest of the family follows, uncovering action-packed mystery along the way.

ADVENTURES OF THE NORTHWOODS · by Lois Walfrid Johnson
Kate O'Connell and her stepbrother Anders encounter mystery and adventure in northwest Wisconsin near the turn of the century.

AN AMERICAN ADVENTURE SERIES · by Lee Roddy
Hildy Corrigan and her family must overcome danger and hardship during the Great Depression as they search for a "forever home."

BLOODHOUNDS, INC. · by Bill Myers
Hilarious, hair-raising suspense follows brother-and-sister detectives Sean and Melissa Hunter in these madcap mysteries with a message.

GIRLS ONLY! · by Beverly Lewis
Four talented young athletes become fast friends as together they pursue their Olympic dreams.

MANDIE BOOKS · by Lois Gladys Leppard
With over five million sold, the turn-of-the-century adventures of Mandie and her many friends will keep readers eager for more.

PROMISE OF ZION · by Robert Elmer
Following WWII, thirteen-year-old Dov Zalinsky leaves for Palestine—the one place he may still find his parents—and meets the adventurous Emily Parkinson. Together they experience the dangers of life in the Holy Land.

THE RIVERBOAT ADVENTURES · by Lois Walfrid Johnson
Libby Norstad and her friend Caleb face the challenges and risks of working with the Underground Railroad during the mid–1800s.

TRAILBLAZER BOOKS · by Dave and Neta Jackson
Follow the exciting lives of real-life Christian heroes through the eyes of child characters as they share their faith with others around the world.

THE TWELVE CANDLES CLUB · by Elaine L. Schulte
When four twelve-year-old girls set up a business of odd jobs and baby-sitting, they uncover wacky adventures and hilarious surprises.

THE YOUNG UNDERGROUND · by Robert Elmer
Peter and Elise Andersen's plots to protect their friends and themselves from Nazi soldiers in World War II Denmark guarantee fast-paced action and suspenseful reads.

*(ages 8–13)